THE VETALA

THE VETALA

A novel of undying love

PHILLIP ERNEST

Copyright © 2018 Phillip Ernest

All rights reserved. No part of this book may be reproduced, for any reason or by any means, without permission in writing from the publisher.

The following is a work of fiction. Many of the locations are real, although not necessarily as portrayed, but all characters and events are fictional and any resemblance to actual events or people, living or dead, is purely coincidental.

Cover design by Debbie Geltner
Prepared for the press by Kodi Scheer
Book design by WildElement.ca
Printed and bound in Canada.

Library and Archives Canada Cataloguing in Publication

Ernest, Phillip, author
        The vetala / Phillip Ernest.

Issued in print and electronic formats.
ISBN 978-1-988130-66-8 (softcover).--ISBN 978-1-988130-67-5
(HTML).--ISBN 978-1-988130-68-2 (Kindle).--ISBN 978-1-988130-69-9
(PDF)
        I. Title.
PS8609.R54V48 2018   C813'.6   C2017-906565-3
                                                     C2017-906566-1

The publisher gratefully acknowledges the support of the Government of Canada through the Canada Council for the Arts, the Canada Book Fund, and Livres Canada Books, and of the Government of Quebec through the Société de développement des entreprises culturelles (SODEC).

Linda Leith Publishing
Montreal
www.lindaleith.com

PART ONE

A DEATH
Pune, 2014

That morning the news had come to the Lokmanya Tilak Research Institute that Professor Suresh Kshirasagar, its former librarian, had died the night before and willed it a unique ancient manuscript on the *vetala,* the vampire.

The news was a rare major event in the Institute's sleepy world, which continued at the speed of old India despite the rapid erosion of that India that was going on all around it in the Pune neighbourhood in which it stood. The Institute's older members remembered Kshirasagar well from the days when he had been a daily presence in the library, in committee meetings, and in the tea hut where they gathered several times a day; the younger members, never having even seen him, nevertheless knew him through his enduring reputation for kindness and generosity and a vast but unostentatious knowledge of Sanskrit literature. He had retired some twenty years before, following decades of service during which he met all and became friends with many of the scholars, both Indian and foreign, who continuously passed through Pune's most famous Sanskrit institution. Almost no one had seen him since that time, but everyone knew that he remained active, having been forced into early retirement by a rare disease that confined him to his home not far from the Institute.

There he had continued to work on his annotated translation of this forgotten Sanskrit book, about which nothing was known but its name, and that to only a few: *Amrutajijnasa,* Inquiry into the Undead. He had died before completing it, and in his will had left the manuscript and his unfinished work to the Institute with the condition that it should oversee its completion under the direction of his former student, Professor Nada Marjanovic of the University of Zagreb.

Despite his reclusiveness, a few friends had visited him in his home from time to time over these two decades. He was much reduced, it was said, by his condition—a wasting disease which left him pale and so weak that even sunlight and open air had become an affliction. But he seemed to be sustained by his enduring obsession with his book. Kshirasagar's only collaborators on the work had been Dr. Marjanovic, and, some twenty years before, another Croatian scholar, Zoran Vukovic. Marjanovic came to Pune for two months every year, mainly to work on the text with Kshirasagar. Besides his wife Kamala, no one was closer to the childless old scholar than Nada Marjanovic.

So when, that morning, Kamala Kshirasagar called Professor Vimala Bhave, general secretary of the Institute, to tell her the news of her husband's death, Bhave knew that her first task would be to email Nada. She would then write to Shyamala Phadke, one of her own Ph.D. students at Pune University, asking her to work with Marjanovic on the completion of the translation: Marjanovic herself would decide how many scholars she would need to help her, but Bhave was determined that one of them should be Shyamala, who at twenty-four had already proven herself to be a formidable sanskritist and scholar. It seemed probable that Marjanovic would come to Pune immediately on hearing the news, since it was May, and this was when she normally came, between the end of one academic year and the beginning of the next in September.

Bhave wrote:

> *Dear Nada, I am so sorry to have to tell you that this morning Kamala phoned me with the news that Dr. Kshirasagar died last night, and was cremated at dawn, only five hours ago. Perhaps it will not surprise you to learn that in his will he left the Institute the manuscript of the Amrutajijnasa and his work on it, with the condition that the work should be completed here under your supervision. I will be asking Shyamala Phadke to work with you.*
>
> *Dear Nada, I know you will understand me when I say that it is impossible not to feel a bit of gratitude and relief at Dr. Kshirasagar's death. We both know how terribly he suffered for so long. But we also know how he clung to his life in spite of its painfulness, because he loved his work and knew how important it was. You can live with that best part of him for a while longer. No one is better able to appreciate it than you.*

I look forward to seeing you again soon.

Vimala

She pressed send, then went out and sat on one of the benches in the area between the main building and the library. Months of rainless summer heat had turned the Institute's hermitage-like grounds various shades of brown amidst which the lotus pond, daily replenished by hand, stood out as an oasis of luxuriant green.

The scene before Bhave's eyes had changed little over the course of her long career: it had decayed, it was true, but the world the Institute represented, though dying, was somehow essentially timeless. Kshirasagar had been one of the great figures of its *Kaliyuga,* its Age of Decline, and she knew that many considered her to belong to the same class. There was a new generation that was worthy to succeed them, but they were fewer than ever before, and the present age had little to offer them. Those who could not leave would pass their lives in this fading world, while those who could would flee to universities in England, Germany, America, where the spirit of the old time was in many ways better remembered than it was here. But she at least remembered it, and even younger people like Nada and Shyamala, though they had only seen its dying light, understood it. Something of it would survive for a little while longer.

The flat sound of a metal disc struck with a mallet announced the first tea break, and the scholars, most of them old and slow, began walking from the Institute's several buildings towards the tea hut. Reflected sunlight flashed from the heavy traffic on the roads bordering the Institute, beyond the summer-wasted trees and untamed undergrowth of its large domains. Claimed from a barren hillside on the city's remote periphery more than a century ago, the grounds were now extremely valuable real estate at the centre of a vast urban area. A host of developers were desperate to sweep away this useless cluster of falling-apart old buildings which stood in the way of proud new apartment complexes with pretentious names like Symphony and Monte Ville. A ravenous modernity pressed ever more heavily upon the Institute's borders.

For all Bhave knew, Kshirasagar's translation might be one of its final utterances, one of its last acts of devotion to an ever more deeply forgotten classical past. Bhave didn't know much about the *Amrutajijnasa,* but she knew that a great scholar had dedicated most of his life to it: it must be important, must, like all ancient books that survive, preserve some perennial truth that the present age needed to remember and pass on in its turn. This work of preservation was the work to which Bhave, too, had dedicated her life. Her role in bringing about the completion of Kshirasagar's edition would almost certainly be her own final act of devotion.

The greetings of two colleagues roused her from her meditation, and she got up and joined the slow procession of the Institute's old guard.

Professor Nada Marjanovic stood on the sidewalk of Usha Road, staring at Dr. Kshirasagar's house on the opposite side.

It was her house too, this house named *Yadnya*, Worship. The days she had spent here over the last twenty years and more had been the most precious of her life. This was where she had learned the best part of her life's craft with her most important teacher, where she had been in love for the first and only time, and she and her lover had shared their discovery of the country and literature they adored, while being cherished by Kshirasagar and his wife as if they were their own children. Here Nada had returned to grieve after the unreal trauma that had shattered that beautiful dream, robbed her of her love, crushed and burnt out her ability to love, and hardened her mind into a weapon of vengeance. And this was where Nada had returned to train herself for that revenge.

She couldn't remember how long she had been standing here. People were passing frequently, typical residents of this posh quarter, many of them on their way to the nearby *gymkhana,* and many looked at her, she being perhaps a bit more conspicuous than the usual foreigners, who were not as rare here as they were in the old city across the river. Nada was tall, slender, olive-complexioned, with a narrow, beautiful face, and long black hair drawn back in a ponytail that added to the general impression she gave of being twenty-five instead of forty-five years old. In a sari or Punjabi pantsuit and with the right body language, she easily passed for a fair Indian rather than a *gori,* a white woman, but today she was dressed Western style, in pants, shirt, and a brimmed sun hat, with a large knapsack containing all she needed for her regular trip to her second home, so she was getting the attention due to a striking, unchaperoned white woman who looked like she might not know where she was going.

But of course she knew her way around, better in fact that many of the younger people walking past her. As she always did when she arrived back in India, she had taken an auto-rickshaw, the three-wheeled taxi of Indian cities, from Swargate bus station only as far as College Road, so that she could wade back into *her* India through streets that she had walked, alone or accompanied, for twenty-five years. And this time the need to reconnect was greater than ever, because what had been the most precious surviving thread of that past, going back to its beginning, had been cut.

Nada turned and began to walk slowly through this neighbourhood that was a palimpsest for her. A year ago she had been walking in the opposite direction, towards *Yadnya,* thinking of how close she and Kshirasagar were getting to the heart of the *Amrutajijnasa's* mystery after so many years of slow, careful reading of the text—a mystery epitomized by one of its final verses, whose meaning, the key to the whole book, had been stolen from them by some ancient vandal who had rubbed out its third quarter.

Kshirasagar had been weak, weaker than she'd ever seen him before, but not obviously ailing. He had always known that his illness was degenerative and terminal, so he, Kamala, and Nada had always expected him to get a little worse every year. Last year, Nada had seen that the decline had been sharper than in the past, but she had merely taken this as a sign that he had crossed the threshold of his final phase of life. During those three months, as usual, Nada had lived in her room, sleeping from dawn till noon, doing her own work in and outside of the house until Kshirasagar woke at sundown, and then working with him on the text till sunrise.

The sessions were intensive, but frequently punctuated by talk about other things: Kshirasagar's eighty years lay lightly on him, despite the ravages of his illness, and his interest in his work and the world beyond it remained as vigorous as it ever had been. Kamala ministered to them with tea and meals, and joined their conversation at those times. She was intelligent and educated, but not a sanskritist, so she could not work on the text with them. But she knew the *Amrutajijnasa* as well as anyone could without reading it. She had to: this book had cursed both her husband and her to live like *nishacharis,* night-dwelling demons, and robbed them of the simple happiness they had deserved to share.

Those times, the heart of Nada's life for twenty years...

all over, all gone. She could feel that the loss still wasn't quite real to her, and the reality of it stood behind her like a threatening phantom.

She zigzagged down streets and backstreets, making an indirect way towards the Institute. She stopped at one of the the food stalls in front of Bhandarkar Park to eat a bowl of *bhel,* puffed rice sprinkled with a sauce of chopped tomatoes, onions, and spices—she knew she would be served tea immediately upon sitting down in Bhave's office—then set out for the Institute five minutes away.

In the main office, her arrival was not unexpected. People chatted with her warmly in Marathi—the mother tongue of most people in Pune and the state of Maharashtra—and shared condolences with her about Kshirasagar, dead only a week before. It was noon, and Bhave was sitting at the large table in the Great Hall talking with two southeast Asian Buddhist nuns when Nada walked in.

"Ah, Nada, there you are. I'm just finishing here with these two ladies from Laos who have come to Pune to study Pali. This is Professor Nada Marjanovic from Croatia, a very old friend of all of us at this Institute."

Nada smiled at them, joining her hands in *namaskar,* then sat down at the table while Bhave continued to discuss the nuns' plans with them. One of the Institute's groundskeepers went to prepare tea.

When the nuns were gone, Bhave sighed and said, "Ah Nada, this is usually such a happy day for us, the day of your arrival. It's the end of an age: nothing is going to be the same now that he's gone. And yet the same work has

9

to be completed—without him. That will be painful for you, but it will also be part of your mourning, and when it is finished you will have done your funeral rite for him, and will be ready to move on to the next stage of your life. We'll go and look at the manuscript in a moment."

"How's Kamala?" asked Nada softly, feeling her smile fade a little. She had thought of stopping at *Yadnya* first, as she often did, but upon seeing it had realized that she wasn't quite ready.

"Kamala is all right, not devastated," said Bhave. "Naturally she feels something of the same relief I mentioned to you in my email. But of course her life is all of a sudden profoundly empty. I don't know what it can hold for her after this. I think Dr. Kshirasagar, too, worried about that, and that may have been one of the reasons that he wanted the manuscript to be taken out of the house as soon as he died."

They sat in silence for a while. Then Nada said: "We will very probably get a visit from Avinash Chandrashekhar, and soon."

Bhave looked at her, apparently mystified.

"He will know," said Nada, answering her implicit question, her voice quavering just a little. "He always does. You don't know everything about the *Amrutajijnasa* and its history, but you know it's complex, and... terrible, and you know that Avinash Chandrashekhar has always been deeply involved in it—for longer than any of us, actually. I don't like having to come out and say it, and you probably don't need me to, but... he isn't a good person."

Bhave winced and looked down, as if simultaneously registering her shock at such a bold statement and her tacit acknowledgment of its truth.

"He's going to want very desperately to seize the manuscript, even though he can't actually touch it," Nada went on impetuously. "He has always known that Dr. Kshirasagar had it, but he couldn't get near him, because Kshirasagar was too... *noble*—I can't explain. But he doesn't fear me the way he feared him, so the manuscript is more vulnerable now. It must be kept locked up with the other most valuable ones."

Nada felt herself growing agitated, giddy with anxiety, grief, lack of sleep. She was aware that she was talking too fast, saying things that wouldn't make sense to Bhave, and that Bhave was looking at her with concern. But these were things that needed to be said, somehow, and right away.

"We should even consider the possibility of me doing this work in Kshirasagar's house itself," she said. "This would make sense: everything we ever used in the study of the text over more than twenty years, every book, manuscript, and piece of correspondence with other scholars, is in Dr. Kshirasagar's study in *Yadnya.* And it would be better, it would be *safer,* for it to stay in a space where so much good work has been done, where so much merit has been generated."

"We will consider this," said Bhave, clearly trying to sound reassuring. "We have a very free hand. This is not like other projects of the Institute: everyone knows that this was your work with Kshirasagar, and no one is wanting to take control of it and refashion it according to his own ideas. The board will not reject any of our requests. Dr. Kshirasagar willed the manuscript to the Institute because he wanted it to be in safe hands, not because he needed it to be in this building itself. And I know, Nada, that he considered the safest hands to be yours. But he couldn't very well have willed the manuscript to you, a foreigner—with the attitudes of some people being what they are. Its existence was known. People would have wondered where it had ended up—and they would have guessed."

"Yes... yes, *you're* right about all this, of course," said Nada, allowing herself to sound more confident than she really felt. Bhave smiled demonstratively.

The groundskeeper returned with two teas on a tray, and Bhave and Nada sat for a while sipping them in silence. Then Bhave said: "I don't think you've met Shyamala Phadke, the young scholar I'm proposing to you as a partner in this project. I don't think you'll need anyone besides her to help you with the editing and translation—if you need any help at all, for that matter."

"Oh, help would be welcome," said Nada, *"if* it's really help. But if the person isn't up to the mark, you know, she'll just be getting in the way. And the mark is extremely high, in this case, because she will in effect be replacing Kshirasagar."

"Of course, no one can replace Kshirasagar," said Bhave decisively, nodding side-to-side and making a gesture of dismissal with her right hand, both characteristically Indian movements, "but I'm proposing her to you because, young though she is, she is the only scholar I can think of who shows signs of one day being able to reach Kshirasagar's level. She's only twenty-four, but she's already been around the Institute for almost ten years. I'm now guiding her at the university in her Ph.D. thesis on Bana's *Kadambari,* which is of course an extremely difficult literary text. She's very smart, and I also think that she has the right kind of fresh and unprejudiced mentality for the job. She'll be here this afternoon. Perhaps you'll remember having seen her before."

"Well..." said Nada, unable to completely conceal her skepticism, "if *you're* so impressed with her, I look forward to meeting her myself."

"Ah, that reminds me," Bhave said with a new cheerfulness. "I received an email from our old friend Saul Levitt a couple of days ago."

Nada felt a wave of pleasure and surprise that swept away her memory of the troubled present.

Bhave beamed at Nada, and went on: "He says he'll be here in a few weeks, in July and August, staying in the guest house, as usual. I thought of him just now because it did actually cross my mind that *he* could collaborate with you on this work. But I immediately realized that he would not be the right person. Saul is very brilliant, as we know, and he can do anything he puts his mind to. But he's a loner, he goes his own way, and he is always busy with so many of his own projects. So I'm certain that such a collaborative task would not interest him. But I knew

13

that you would be happy to hear that he'll be here soon."

"Yes, indeed," said Nada rather softly. "I love Saul. We all do."

Bhave finished her tea, and said, "Let's go now and have a look at the manuscript."

They got up and went from the Great Hall into the south wing, which housed the manuscriptorium. Shelves piled with red cloth-bound manuscripts—most of them unknown, even by title, to anyone now working at the Institute—were visible behind the glass faces of tall heavy wooden cabinets, as old as the Institute itself, which stood in rows in the centre of the room. Similar locked cabinets against the wall contained the more valuable collections, and a tall windowless iron cabinet in one corner was for the most precious manuscripts—precious enough, in terms of money or historical importance, that someone might conceivably want to steal them. Despite being a tall room furnished with windows on all sides, the manuscriptorium was a dark dungeon-like space, heavy with constantly accumulating dust which sat ready to rise in clouds from objects that escaped the desultory attention of dusters for more than a couple of days. On the walls, pictures eighty, ninety, and a hundred years old showed the great scholars of the Institute's first generation sitting on the very same heavy, throne-like wooden chairs that its members still used every day.

On one side of the room, separated by low wooden dividers, was the office of Dr. Gajanan Ekbote, one of the Institute's senior scholars and officers. He rose from his desk when he saw Bhave and Nada, and joined his hands in *namaskar* to greet Nada.

"Nada just now arrived," said Bhave. "We're here to see the manuscript."

Ekbote went over to the iron cabinet, lifted a set of keys that was chained to his belt, isolated one, and slipped it into the keyhole. The door creaked open, revealing four shelves piled with the familiar red bundles, and a shelf dedicated to one bundle alone. This he took out with a carefulness suited to the handling of a living thing, and going and placing it on his desk, untied the cloth cords and opened the red cloth, revealing a neat stack of darkened palm leaf pages of about the length and breadth of a shoebox. Within a broad margin, each page contained a perfect rectangle of lines written without spaces in still-black ink, with a few words in red here and there. The hand was neat and elegant, and as Nada knew, the text was almost totally free of errors, the writer having used white paint to correct most of the few he had made. Script, writing materials, and language all indicated that this manuscript must have been produced somewhere in the vicinity of modern Mysore around the thirteenth century. This was the only known copy of the *Amrutajijnasa,* and was thus possibly the author's own autograph.

Nada felt her heart fill with emotion as she looked at these pages that they had so loved and deeply known over so many years, she and the beloved teacher and friend just now departed, and the long-dead lover who had paid with his life for innocently rousing the evil therein described;

pages that went back to the hand of a mysterious author who called himself Amruteshvara—"lord of the divine nectar," or "master of the undead"—who had somehow known this evil intimately, and written to teach the world how to protect itself from it.

Nada's breath caught softly, and Ekbote looked up. "Ah Nada," he said, visibly touched, "the manuscript is yours; you will even have a key to this cabinet, if you want. It's just that it must be kept as secure as possible; that's why Dr. Kshirasagar wanted it kept here. You understand that even better than we can. In fact, I have no doubt that his main reason for willing it to the Institute was to keep it safe until you arrived."

Nada recovered herself, rapidly palming away the tears of a moment before, and said, "Yes, I think he may have had something like that in mind. Indeed, we may move it back to *Yadnya.* I'll be staying there from tonight. Personally, I would feel much safer keeping and working on it there. I want to see how it feels, how *safe* it feels, being there again... now that he's gone."

"Dr. Kshirasagar's work is also here, on the same shelf," said Ekbote, pointing to a string-bound stack of notebooks about a foot tall.

Nada said, "The work that I and Miss Phadke will be doing will have two parts: First, we'll be making an electronic copy of all the final text so far produced of the translation and commentary; I would have begun to do this this year anyway, since we had almost reached the final chapter. Second, we'll be completing the writing of

the translation and commentary. The first part we can begin immediately, here; the second... our course will be
clearer once I talk with Mrs. Kshirasagar. For now, I want
to leave something with the manuscript which I think
may make it a little safer, though the mere fact that it was
in Dr. Kshirasagar's hands for so long is probably more
than enough to protect it."

She took off her knapsack, put it on a nearby writing desk, and took from one of the inner pockets an
akshamala—a rosary of eleocarpus seeds—which Dr.
Kshirasagar had given her when she and her lover Zoran
had first stayed with them ages ago; such a concentrated
symbol of the bond of affection between her and that
good man would be an exceptionally powerful deterrent
to the creature who had so hated him, she thought. She
then re-wrapped the manuscript, and tied the *akshamala*
into the knot of the cloth strings.

"This can go back now," she said, "and yes, I would
feel better if I could have one of the keys to this cabinet."

Ekbote went behind the dividers to his desk, opened
a drawer, and came back with the key. Putting it into the
knapsack pocket from which she had taken the rosary,
Nada said, "Thank you both so much for your help and
understanding—I can feel that you understand. I'm suddenly so tired... the journey... I actually need to lie down
right away."

"Let me give you the key to one of the rooms in the
guest house," said Bhave.

"No," Nada replied, "thank you, but I'm afraid if I

lie down on a bed I'd be out cold till morning. I'll just take a nap on the verandah in front of one of the vacant rooms. I'm still not too old to rough it a bit," she smiled. "It won't be the first time."

She went out into the heavy afternoon heat through the south wing's door, which still bore the marks of the major event in the Institute's recent history: a decade before, a mob of fanatics from a right-wing cultural group had ransacked the library and tried unsuccessfully to force their way into the main building, having been whipped into a fury by a local demagogue who had denounced the Institute for its collaboration with foreign sanskritists. Yes, she thought, this new xenophobia, one of the social effects of the country's rapid economic development and increasing prominence on the world stage, must have played a role in Kshirasagar's decision to bequeath the manuscript to the Institute. Willing it to her would have been completely self-defeating, since their work on it could not be completed outside of India, and in any case had no meaning there; and the suspicion that he had given away a precious piece of the ancient national past to a foreigner would have endangered both her and it. And it wasn't hard to imagine why he hadn't broached the subject with her, as the end drew palpably nearer: she wouldn't have listened, she couldn't have faced it.

She walked to the guest house, a late nineteenth-century two-storey building with six rooms and a central hall on the first floor and two larger apartments on the second. Circumambulating it, she saw that all the

first-floor rooms were padlocked—another sign of decline, she thought: twenty years ago the guest house had
always been full of visiting Indian and foreign scholars,
though as the years passed and the Institute's standards
and esteem dwindled, more and more of the guests were
students from poorer Asian countries who had come
to Pune to study English or engineering at the university or one of the many colleges nearby. She and Zoran
had stayed here twice for extended periods in one of
the upstairs apartments. They were both already close
to Kshirasagar at that time, but their intense premari-
tal sex life would have been too embarrassing even for
the relatively liberal doctor and his wife, and so they
had taken the room here as a place to pass the nights.

The grief that attached to this building for Nada was
itself more than twenty years old, by now an ancient and
rarely noticed essence of her being; but this new loss, so
intimately joined to it, had re-disturbed it, thrusting her
back into its embrace, stirring the memories that haunted
these scenes, drawing her back to them with a reawakened
awareness of what lay beneath their surface.

So she stood before this house, too, as she had stood
before *Yadnya* a couple of hours before, absorbed in a
dream of memory and reawakening emotion. But the
emotion was still too deep and sluggish with disuse to express itself in tears; instead, it attached itself to the physical
exhaustion that was already mastering her. She almost
stumbled up the concrete steps to the first-floor verandah,
took off her knapsack and put it on the stone floor in front

of room number three, and lay on her back with her knapsack as her pillow, in the shade, in the silence of the Institute's grounds, with the soft prattle of traffic beyond, and immediately sank into a slumber whispering with inchoate images of the past, by turns comforting and ominous.

The next day Nada and her new colleague Shyamala were
in the south wing working at wooden desks in adjacent
cubicles. It was eleven o'clock, and heavy sunlight slanted
onto the stone sills of the east-facing windows, while the
traffic on Malati Road flashed and rumbled beyond the
trees in front of the main building. Shyamala was entering
Dr. Kshirasagar's handwritten translation and notes into
her laptop, and Nada was reading through the untrans-
lated final chapter.

At *Yadnya* the night before, Nada had realized that
there was every reason for the manuscript to be taken back
to the house where this work had always been done. Kamala needed her there, and Nada had strongly felt the protecting power that the text and its devotees had invested
that space with over so many years. She would initiate this
process of relocation today. Kamala had readily agreed,
saying that Bhave and Ekbote had come to the house on
the afternoon after Kshirasagar's cremation to take the
manuscript to the Institute, and at that time, Kamala had
felt glad to be relieved of its inauspicious presence. With
her husband gone, Kamala revealed to Nada that she no

21

longer felt safe alone in the house with it. But with Nada there, Kamala confessed that she felt no fear—Nada was, really, the only source of joy in her life anymore—and the newly widowed woman looked forward to the consolation of having her surrogate daughter there with her all day, like in old times, instead of at the Institute.

Nada had loved Shyamala immediately—a strong, independent, driven young woman who reminded her of her younger self. Bespectacled and dressed in a Punjabi pantsuit, Shyamala had the surface appearance of a typically demure Tilak Institute girl, but her long unbound hair and a certain unapologetic confidence in her eyes suggested that beneath the surface she might not be quite what she seemed—and this was in fact true, as Nada quickly learned during their first, almost schoolgirlishly vivacious conversation.

Shyamala represented a newer strain. She had gone to an English rather than a Marathi school, where she had learned German as well, but unlike most of her English-educated colleagues, she had taken a serious interest in the intellectual realms opened to her by these Western languages, without forgetting that Marathi and Hindi were her mother tongues, and that they were more than just instruments of everyday business, having long literary traditions of their own. Her parents were academicians from traditional but liberal Sanskrit-knowing Brahmin families which had in the past produced many social reformers and Freedom Fighters in the struggle against the British. They had raised their daughter, as they would have raised a son, to feel that life was hers for the taking, and had not sought to have more children after her. At twenty-four she was unmarried, but was not waiting until her thirties, like most of her less modern contemporaries, to find a possible mate: to their quiet scandal, she had a boyfriend, and by their behaviour with each other the two of them gave no reason to think that they were saving themselves for marriage. Nada couldn't have dared to hope for a more sympathetic companion in her present work, and very soon came to feel that she had found not only a brilliant junior colleague, but probably also a lifelong friend.

One of the groundskeepers came and told them in Marathi, "Bhave Madam has called you."

"This is it," thought Nada, and took a deep breath, preparing herself for what she expected to be the first round of a new agon with her old enemy. She and Shyamala got up and walked with the groundskeeper through the manuscriptorium and Great Hall into the north wing.

When they came into Dr. Bhave's office, Nada saw her at her desk with three senior scholars (two men and a woman) seated to her right and a man of about Nada's age sitting across from her. He was dressed in shirt, pants, and jacket, which covered what seemed to be a lean but muscular build. His hair was long and tied back, his skin dark, his face round but clearly sculpted, with a broad nose, full lips, and large but narrowed eyes which shone with a smoldering attentiveness. As soon as Nada entered, he stood to a height of over six feet, held out his hand to her, and smiled, revealing large and perfect teeth that chilled

23

the warmth the smile seemed intended to convey. Nada kept her expression unchanged as she accepted his hand.

"You must be Dr. Marjanovic," he said in a rich voice with the slight accent of the English-educated speaker of Kannada, the language of the southern state of Karnataka. "What I mean, of course," he continued, beamingly addressing the whole room without taking his eyes off Nada, "is that Nada must be Dr. Marjanovic by now, since of course we are very well acquainted, but have not seen each other since she was still writing her dissertation for the University of Zagreb."

Nada nodded and did not smile, holding his hard stare with her own, then looking towards Bhave. "Dr. Chandrashekhar and I knew each other well, years ago," said Nada, "but we've been out of touch since then. I'm not too surprised to be meeting him again in these circumstances. We've both been on the trail of the *vetala* all our academic lives, though we've been coming at him from somewhat different directions. It was inevitable that our paths would cross again, sooner or later."

"That our paths would cross! You make it sound like such an unfriendly business!" he laughed.

Then he spoke in Sanskrit, fiercely and harshly, and so rapidly that the other Indians, unused to the conversational use of the language, could not catch it. Without missing a beat, Nada replied equally rapidly and in the same tone, raising her defiant eyes to meet his. She felt a shudder of confusion go through the room: Western sanskritists who could speak the language at all, let alone

24

fluently, were extremely rare. Their exchange had in fact consisted of nothing more than a formal greeting on each side, but the manner in which they had spoken suggested the violence of a personal quarrel.

Avinash held her gaze with what looked like the mingled mockery and admiration of an old enemy, then continued: "But I have to confess, there is unfortunately a slight element of conflict in the circumstances that bring us together again today. I am here as the representative of the Dharmika Sahitya Research Institute of Mysore, whose name will be familiar to all of you. Dr. Kshirasagar's will has revealed the fate of an extremely important manuscript that went missing from the Institute's library in 1986. We naturally assume that it came into the good doctor's hands in a completely innocent fashion, but now that its whereabouts have been revealed, we want it back. It is ours: the Tilak Oriental Research Institute has no legal or moral right to it, and we expect that it will immediately be handed over."

Bhave looked shocked at this, and seemed to be about to say something, but Nada spoke first, having fully rehearsed herself for every possible contingency that this scene might present. "Dr. Kshirasagar received the manuscript as a gift from Dr. Kashyap, who was then the Dharmika Sahitya Research Institute's librarian; this is documented by a letter that Dr. Kayshyap wrote at the time, and that came to the Institute along with the manuscript and Dr. Kshirasagar's translation and notes. It's only right that you should read it for yourself," she said, looking at Avinash, "now that it surprisingly turns out that someone is evidently suspicious of the gift—surprisingly, because this is the first I've heard of any such suspicion, and as you know I knew Dr. Kshirasagar well, and began studying this text with him more than twenty years ago. In fact, Dr. Chandrashekhar, I've also known you for almost exactly the same length of time, and this is the first time you've mentioned anything about such a theft." She felt adrenalized by her confidence in the strength of her argument. Avinash's bid was clumsy, clearly desperate. She knew he would leave this room having gained nothing.

"Dr. Kashyap did not own the manuscripts in the library, and had no right to give any of them away," replied Avinash sharply. "No one would have allowed him to do this if he had told anyone about it. The fact that he didn't tell anyone suggests that at that point he was mentally not quite the man he had been, and indeed there was other evidence of that. The matter was an embarrassment to the Institute, but Dr. Kashyap was influential, and so when it was found that the manuscript was missing, the board of directors decided to simply let the matter drop instead of creating a scandal by raising the issue with him. Now that both the participants in this criminal transaction are dead, and the location of the book has been revealed by the death of the second, there are no tender feelings left to spare. It is ours. Give it back."

Nada turned to Dr. Bhave. "Doctor, I can assure you that the construction that Dr. Chandrashekhar is putting on these events is not right. But surely the first thing we should do is look at the letter itself." She turned to look at Avinash, almost with an arrogant toss of the head, conscious that a mocking expectation of her imminent victory must be plainly written in her face.

"Yes, that makes sense," said Bhave. "Shyamala, would you please go and bring the letter along with the manuscript itself?"

Avinash looked alarmed and confused, and Nada suppressed a smile of excited satisfaction: as she had hoped, he hadn't anticipated this possibility. He had unwittingly delivered himself into her hands.

She quickly replied, "Let me get it, Dr. Bhave," and hurried out before Avinash could object.

She half-ran through the Great Hall to the manuscriptorium, opened the iron cabinet, found the folder containing the letter in the pile of notebooks, and took the folder and the manuscript back to Bhave's office.

When Avinash saw Nada with the red cloth-bound bundle under her arm, the confusion in his eyes became panic. Nada put it down on Bhave's desk, and carefully took the laminated letter out of the folder. It was written in Sanskrit; she read it aloud, then offered it to Avinash, but he was still staring at the manuscript on the desk, and did not put out his hand to accept it.

"You can take a copy of this back with you," she said, turning and putting it back in the folder. "You're also free to examine the manuscript, if you have any reason to. In fact, why don't you join the research team? You are after all one of the leading experts in the literature on the *vetala,* if not *the* leading expert. I actually really like that idea. We need you."

She carefully, lovingly picked up the bundle of red, and kept her eyes on him as she began to move towards him, smiling slightly, making an effort not to burst out laughing at the brilliant absurdity of her offer, which he could not conceivably accept. "There are just so many things in here that I'd love to show you, that no one else would understand..."

Avinash stepped back and stood with his back against the bare concrete wall, looking like he was trying to avoid cringing. "There's no point in my looking at it here," he said in an almost strangled voice. "But I may well take you up on your offer—I will. The project should as much as possible be in the hands of Indians, anyway. I can think of some cultural organizations and politicians who would be very interested to know that the Institute is again favouring foreign scholars over Indian ones."

He glared at her, and she knew that if he had been reduced to making such empty threats, she had won: the Institute would face no legal challenge from the Dharmika Sahitya Research Institute—if Avinash was even really associated with it at all.

Bhave shook her head sadly and said, "I know Dr. Chandrashekhar is only talking like this because he is angry. But although the book is staying with us, he is indeed most welcome to join the project if he wishes. It will do honour to the final wish of Dr. Kshirasagar to have another esteemed expert working on the text to which he devoted so many years of his life." She gave Nada a look that suggested she knew what was going on.

"I'll talk to my institute about this," said Avinash. "They won't be happy to hear about the result of this meeting, but if we can't get our property back then I should at least be involved in the work as the Institute's representative."

He moved quickly towards the door, and without turning to look at them, muttered *"Punar darśanāya"*—a Sanskrit "we'll meet again"—in a threatening tone, and left.

"Well!" said Nada, looking at Shyamala, "I think this meeting has been sufficiently distressing that we'll need at least some tea before we're ready to go back to work. Let's go across the street to the Hutatma." She turned to Bhave and the three senior scholars, who like Shyamala were looking a little shaken and confused, as if the first shattering thunderstorm of the monsoon had just passed, leaving behind a sky suddenly clear and serene again. She felt a little sorry for them, but in the exhilaration of her victory was unable to suppress an almost mischievous smile. She bowed slightly, said *"Punar darśanāya!"*, and looking meaningfully into Shyamala's incredulously laughing eyes, walked out of the room with her.

The Hutatma Hotel at the corner of Malati Road and Tilak Institute Road was an old-fashioned vegetarian restaurant of a kind that had been more common in the Institute's neighbourhood before the creeping modernization of recent years had begun to pick them off, replacing them with posher, more expensive restaurants and coffee shops, some of them international chains, which catered to the rich kids attending the neighbourhood's many colleges and preparation academies. Like the Institute itself, the Hutatma was becoming an anachronism; the Institute's employees, especially the younger ones, had always hung out there, but it was rapidly coming to seem more of a refuge than a hangout.

"I've always loved this place, and I've always loved its name," said Nada: "Hutatma, 'the self-sacrificing'. Quite a heavy name for a restaurant—and more appropriate for a non-vegetarian one, wouldn't you think?"

Shyamala laughed.

They went in and sat down, and when tea came, Shyamala said, "A frightening character, this Chandrashekhar. I've heard of him before. His family has produced many famous scholars. He's never worked at the Institute, but he's appeared here from time to time over the years. Dr. Kshirasagar knew him, they say, and there was some kind of history between them—not good, I think."

Nada looked down. She had thought ahead about this conversation too, but in this case, she still wasn't sure what she was going to say.

"But I was a bit surprised that he seemed to know you so well," said Shyamala.

"We go back... a long way," said Nada. "I knew him both in Europe and here in India. We aren't friends, just in case that wasn't obvious. When I was still an M.Phil. student at the University of Zagreb, he came to attend our conference on *vetalashastra,* literature on vampires.

He was doing his Ph.D. at the University of Bonn, also on *vetalashastra*—an incredible coincidence, because at that time *no one* was studying *vetalashastra,* not in Europe, not in India. It wasn't even a recognized area of study in indology—we intended the conference to address just that.

"So... it was very, very interesting to meet Avinash Chandrashekhar. He was a couple of years older than me—than us, me and my partner Zoran, partner in work, partner in life: we were going to be married."

"Ah," said Shyamala with sympathy and surprise, and what might even have been a touch of guilt for having broached what was beginning to sound like it must be a traumatic subject.

Nada allowed her face to register a grateful acknowledgement, and she continued.

"Yes, Avinash Chandrashekhar: he had the tremendous advantages that conservative southern Brahmins bring to the field. His family, you may know, was the typical hybrid, with feet firmly planted in both the past and the present: very orthodox, very learned, but at the same time thoroughly modern, in other ways. Some of his relatives are traditional scholars and priests, some are university professors (and not just of Sanskrit), some are IT professionals."

Shyamala nodded. "I know the type."

"Don't we all!" laughed Nada. "And don't we all admire and fear people like him." Shyamala smiled in an "I hear you" kind of way, and Nada felt, as she often did, a surge of affection for the younger woman, so kindred to her in intellect and spirit.

"So he was raised to be a *pandita*," said Nada, "a traditional Sanskrit scholar—Sanskrit is as much his first language as Kannada is. But in adolescence he rebelled, deciding to go into academic Sanskrit studies instead—actually not a very grave rebellion, in such a family."

"Indeed," said Shyamala. "They say the South Asian Studies departments of American universities are full of people like him."

"That's true," said Nada, "and I'm sure you'll see that for yourself someday.

"So, at Bonn he was writing his Ph.D. under Professor Virgiliu Munteanu, a great Romanian scholar. But you could almost say that, in a sense, Munteanu was studying under *him*, since Chandrashekhar came to Bonn with the text he was determined to work on. When applying, he had said he was going to write his dissertation on the *vetala* in Sanskrit literature, but when he got to Bonn, he showed Munteanu this manuscript he'd brought with him, a totally unknown text titled *Vetalaviveka*— 'Definition of the Vampire,' something like that. Munteanu was completely fascinated: the *vetala* described in this text (as in ours, the *Amrutajijnasa*) was in so many ways the vampire he knew from his own childhood in Romania—and we know him in Croatia, too."

"Oh... right," said Shyamala. "Croatia is close to... Transylvania! Isn't it?"

Nada laughed, and so did Shyamala, perhaps a little relieved to see that she hadn't inadvertently offended her.

"Yes, you're absolutely right," said Nada. "So, yes, it was very exciting to meet Chandrashekhar at the conference. When we organized it—Zoran, and I, and our Ph.D. supervisor Professor Dragan Klobucar—we thought the *Amrutajijnasa* was the only text of its kind, and that therefore no one else was likely to be studying *vetalas,* since of course the previously known Sanskrit literature on *vetalas* is not very substantial. We had the text of the *Amrutajijnasa*—a copy of it—that Kshirasagar had shared with Professor Klobucar, and we thought that was all there was. That was our first exposure to this book that was to become so important in our lives, and our introduction to Dr. Kshirasagar, who had met Klobucar in Pune.

"The conference was small: a few scholars and graduate students from European and North American universities presented papers. But naturally what we really wanted to hear was Chandrashekhar's paper. And it didn't disappoint: it was a revelation. It made it sound like his book, the *Vetalaviveka,* was very similar to our *Amrutajijnasa,* and contained most of the same types of matter, but not as fully treated. The main difference was that it lacked anything corresponding to the *Amrutajijnasa's* final chapter, *Amrutashamana,* 'Killing the Undead'—or more precisely, *putting the undead to rest,* giving them peace.

"When Zoran delivered our paper, which focused mainly on the difficulties of understanding this final chapter, Avinash seemed beside himself with some kind of rage."

"Somehow... I don't find that too hard to imagine," said Shyamala, laughing a little uncomfortably.

"Right," said Nada. "That's exactly how he was acting. While Zoran was reading, Avinash sat listening, but his eyes were wild, furious. The question period after the paper ended up being longer than the presentation itself. Avinash was the only questioner. Zoran (who was a more advanced sanskritist than me) did most of the talking, with me and Professor Klobucar contributing from time to time.

"Naturally Avinash's questions were fascinating to us. We learned as much from him as he did from us, since he was able to cast light on many points in the text that had been obscure to us—though some of that light later turned out to be deceptive. He was particularly eager—*very* eager—to know about the final chapter. He had so many strong opinions about how the obscure passages in it should be interpreted—and in particular the book's great mystery, the verse near the very end which reveals the one thing which the *vetala*-killer must know, without which no method of killing him can be effective. That verse is defective in our text. The third quarter is missing: the palm leaf has been rubbed through at that point—deliberately, without a doubt, because the rest of the text is almost entirely intact."

Nada smiled playfully. "Have you read ahead?"

Shyamala looked embarrassed.

"I hope you have!" laughed Nada. "So maybe you've found it already:

na śastreṇa na śāstreṇa nihantuṃ śakyate 'mṛtaḥ

Not by weapon, not by lore can the undead be killed.

And then there's the missing quarter, and then the end of the verse:

mumukṣuṃ śamayet tu tam

... one can lay to rest him who longs for release.

"Avinash insisted that the missing quarter must have mentioned some kind of weapon or poison. We had thought of that, since it's the obvious supposition, but I had always had a feeling that that couldn't be right, because the preceding part of the chapter lists and describes those things. This verse had to be unique: it comes at the end of the chapter, like the key to the whole thing. And it seems obvious that someone else, at some time, also thought it was special—special enough that it couldn't be allowed to survive unmutilated."

They sat for a while, sipping their now lukewarm tea for the first time.

"So what happened then?" asked Shyamala. "You must have begun to collaborate, all of you in Zagreb and Chandrashekhar and his guide in Bonn?"

"That would only have made sense, wouldn't it," said Nada, "but it didn't happen that way. In Zagreb, Avinash and his guide Munteanu said that we would get together, compare the texts, work together on the *Amrutajijnasa,* our book, the problematic one. Munteanu seemed really excited, and no wonder, but it was obvious that Avinash was reluctant. I could still see that mysterious fury in him, like he was indignant at having to *share* the *Amrutajijnasa* with anyone, even though we had it and he didn't. That's the way it had felt during the question period: he wasn't *asking,* he was *demanding what was his.*

"When he got back to Bonn he wrote to us asking for his own copy of the manuscript, but we wouldn't do that... Scholarly jealousy—not at all towards Avinash and Munteanu, but it's just dangerous to have a copy of a unique and important text floating around out there when you're still trying to uncover the heart of its mystery. So we told him that work on the *Amrutajijnasa* would have to happen in Zagreb. He wrote back that we would arrange such collaborative sessions in the future, and in the meantime we would keep one another informed about our work on our respective texts. But we never heard from him, to the disappointment of everyone else, including Professor Munteanu."

"So that's the whole story?" asked Shyamala. "I'm ... surprised. It doesn't seem to explain the *bitterness* I felt between the two of you when you met in Bhave's office. I'm sorry, but it's difficult not to mention what I noticed, since we're talking about this now."

"No, don't worry, I'm not a private person," said Nada. "There *is* more to tell, more *did* happen later—here in India. Maybe I'll tell you about that too, sometime. It would explain the bitterness. But it's a very strange story, difficult to tell. And even more difficult to believe." She let her gaze drop to her now almost empty cup. "Sometimes, I'm not even sure that I can quite believe it myself."

Shyamala looked a little embarrassed at the intimate direction the conversation had taken.

"Don't worry," Nada said again, looking up and giving her a reassuring smile. "But let's finish here and get back to the Institute. I haven't yet readjusted to Indian time," she laughed, alluding to the notoriously leisurely pace of all kinds of business in India, "so, you know, I'm actually still in quite a hurry to finish as much as possible today."

The bill was brought, placed as usual on top of a little steel dish of anise seed breath-freshener. Nada put two ten-rupee notes in the dish and sprinkled some of the seeds on them, and they went out into the street blazing with the heat of May.

THE ROAD
January-February 1992

Those weeks with Zoran on the road in Maharashtra and Karnataka had been the best days of Nada's life. They started off together from the Institute's guest house not long after dawn one late January morning, when they could still see their breath. The sun's first touch through the trees was still sweet, not the iron beam of heat it would be by ten o'clock, when they would begin to cling to the shrinking shadows of the roadside as they passed through the thinning suburbs and into the open countryside. The theoretical ultimate goal was Bengaluru a thousand kilometres to the south, but they never really expected to get that far before they had had enough and gotten on a train back to Pune in some village, at some point weeks in the future.

Weeks: they looked forward to weeks of loving each other, of loving India, of walking its country roads through the still savage winter heat of day, and passing the icy nights wrapped in blankets and each other's arms in some field or deserted temple precinct, amidst the profound country silence touched by the voices of crickets and frogs. Sometimes they would stay in a village hotel, if they could convince the proprietors that they were legitimately married in the country they came from; and they could usually convince them, if only thanks to the admiration and amusement they inspired with their earnest but often bizarre Marathi and Kannada when they tried to explain why they didn't have the same family name, or why they hadn't brought their marriage certificate with them. And the fact that they were good-looking didn't hurt, either—the perfect foreign couple from Indians' most generous fantasies about foreigners. Some hotels (or their proprietors) were so grim that they didn't feel safe making love there, and usually when they slept in the fields they were too threatened by the cold to do anything more than cling to each other, reluctant to separate even as much as they would need to in order to open their clothes. But they did so often enough anyway, because they were young and beautiful, and unspeakably happy to be here together. It was a very unusual undertaking, really, arduous and possibly dangerous, as they fully knew. Few Westerners, whether scholars or adventurers, could have thought of it, and even fewer would have dared. But Nada and Zoran were very unusual, and bold. For them, this was the most natural way to love each other in the land they loved.

From Pune they headed south, as much as possible avoiding highways and cities, sticking to unpaved backroads through farmland and countryside. They talked with each other about what they saw and knew, practiced their Sanskrit with each other and their Marathi and Kannada with people they met on the road, ate in the grimy little restaurants of the villages, and once, when they were forced one evening to cross the main highway, at a big shiny one intended mainly as a stop for intercity busses, where they somewhat scandalized the affluent Indian travellers with their vagabond grunginess and lack of a vehicle, and managed to persuade the management to let them use the bus drivers' showers for a price.

Meetings on the road were a joy: the astonishment and delight they inspired even with their limited knowledge of people's mother tongues, the pleasure people took in talking with them and their generosity and patience with their constant mistakes, the things they talked about and learned in these conversations about the humblest, realest things: the lay of the land, locations and distances, food, work, families, marriages.

Over the weeks they built the epic of their personal history, refining it in language and detail as they told and retold it to the men and women with whom they shared the miles or sat resting under roadside trees and temple roofs. People wanted to know everything about them that they knew about themselves and their own *gav* and *desh,* village and country. They tended to assume that they were American, and to be a little mystified when they learned that in fact they were from a small country in eastern Europe where the language was not English. Equally mystifying was the description of their work. Why would a university in this obscure Christian country pay non-Indians to read Sanskrit and teach it to non-Indians?

They were even more surprised when they learned

that they were chiefly interested in *vetalas,* and they had a lot to say on the subject themselves which went far beyond the familiar and limited material found in Sanskrit literature. Village and countryside were swarming with *bhuts* and *prets,* ghouls and ghosts, which watched and influenced everything. Here, Croatians and Indians found their richest common ground, and they could walk for miles comparing their countries' ghoul lores. Because Nada and Zoran were steeped in Eastern European vampirology—once the glory of European superstition, now dying as rapidly as any folk culture. Growing up, they had both spent a lot of time living with grandparents in the countryside, and had taken naturally to those ancient tales and traditions, and as they had entered adolescence, the vampire mythology's themes of tragic love, subliminal sexuality, and alienation had appealed to their sensitive souls. The people they talked with on the road were intensely interested in this strange foreign subspecies of *vetala,* who lived on the blood of the living, slept the day away in his grave, and communicated his living death like a disease to those he fed on, often making it the gift of a dreadful kind of love.

Such meetings were a joy, but they weren't all like this. Sometimes people were mocking and insulting, particularly young men, shouting *he gore* or *he makad*— "Hey whitey! Hey monkey!"—as they sped past on their motorcycles, or inviting Nada to suck or fuck them as they passed them walking in the opposite direction, presumably not expecting them to understand, until Nada, perhaps, replied that, thanks for offering, but eunuchs weren't her type. Once a motorcyclist punched Zoran in the shoulder from behind, then stared him in the face through the rearview mirror as he disappeared down the road ahead, his left fist defiantly raised.

Such experiences reminded them of the risk they had exposed themselves to by undertaking such a long journey on foot through the countryside. Even two young Indians travelling this way would have been in some danger of being instantaneously surrounded, the man beaten and restrained while the woman was gang-raped before his eyes; so how much more vulnerable were they as foreigners, who are always and everywhere in the world easy targets because of their isolation and ignorance—and besides, everyone knows that Americans will fuck anyone and anything, so how could they complain? From time to time, walking or lying together under the splendid icy night sky, they were seized by the chilling certainty that they were being followed and watched; on such nights they would lie face-to-face under their blankets, exhausted but wide awake, clinging more tightly to each other at every innocent snap or rustle from the undergrowth.

But their happiness was rarely interrupted this way, until the meeting that interrupted everything.

One morning, walking into the outskirts of a village, they came to a small roadside temple with three men crouching silently in front, dressed in the standard white cotton farmer's costume of the countryside. The men looked up at them as they passed.

They had just slipped out of Nada's field of vision when one of the three men said, in Croatian, "What did you expect to find here that you couldn't have found at home?"

Nada felt her heart gripped by the cold nausea of fear. She and Zoran stopped, as if moved by the same impulse, and slowly turned to look back at the men. All three were staring up at them—or seemed to be, since the eyes of two of them were white blanks set in the harsh lineaments of their gaunt, sun-baked faces. The third had blazing red irises, and a young man's broad, full-lipped face. Lupine teeth shone in his unsmiling mouth.

For some time Nada and Zoran remained motionless. At last Zoran took two slow steps towards them. "Who are you?" he said in Croatian.

"Fellow travellers," replied the red-eyed one.

Now that they were standing still under its full force, Nada felt her head spinning from the already brutal sun. Things seemed unreal. The man went on, looking at Zoran: "I like your girlfriend. I don't like you. You won't make it out of here alive. But she and I will be seeing each other again." He chuckled darkly, the corners of his fanged mouth turning up in a smile.

Zoran's face twisted with anger. His body almost seemed to swell. Staring murderously at the man, he took one menacing, determined step forward, then staggered, collapsed, sprawled in the dirt before the three men, and lay still. Nada saw the red-eyed one rise, walk around

Zoran, and slowly come towards her as the other two continued to look silently on. Darkness engulfed her. She felt herself fall.

When she came to, she was lying on her side. The sun was touching the horizon. Zoran was still on the ground five feet away from her. The three men were gone, and no one else seemed to be around. She rolled onto her hands and knees and waited for her strength and balance to return. She immediately felt that she had been sexually had, but there was no sense of violation or insemination (she slipped her hand into her pants to check), no injuries or even any sign that her clothes had been disturbed. She crawled over to Zoran, shook him by the shoulder, shouted his name.

His eyes blinked open, then opened wide in terror and confusion. "Nada! What...? Are you all right? Where is he? *Where is he?*" he screamed, scrambling to his hands and knees, his eyes darting in all directions.

Nada held him strongly by the shoulders. "Zoran! Zoran, it's all right! They're gone. They didn't do anything to us. We're all right."

Zoran looked at her in agonized amazement. "Nada! How...? You're... dressed... not hurt..." They were both on their knees, facing each other, and he held her by the shoulders, studying her with wild eyes.

"I'm all right," Nada repeated. "We both fell down, and they must have left. Neither of us has been hurt." She was still confused by the way her body felt, and now she was alarmed by what Zoran was saying. But he looked worryingly unstable, as if he were urgently trying to figure out what was real, and there were no signs that she had been raped, so she resolved to wait and bring the matter up again later.

By now all that remained of the daylight was a smudge on the horizon, and the darkness was deepening around them, checked by the scattered lights of the village houses that grew denser further down the road.

Nada said, "We've got to find someone in the village, eat and drink something, talk to someone, find out if they know who those people were. Obviously we won't go to the police: out here they might be more dangerous to us than the people we just met. We can stay in a hotel in the village, then take a bus out in the morning."

They stood up, holding each other's hands, took a few tentative steps together, then started to walk into the village.

It was at this point that Nada began to notice something extremely strange, something impossible: there was not a living soul anywhere, not on the road, not around the buildings, not in the fields. Lights were on in the houses, the sparse streetlights were lit, but in the ten minutes since they had regained consciousness they had not seen a single person, not seen or even heard a single vehicle. Even the normally omnipresent dogs had vanished. Even insects.

In the village, they passed another, larger temple. They went up to its door, looked into its lit interior, saw at the far end the *lingam,* the phallic idol, decorated with fresh garlands and with incense sticks lit before it. Nada felt the first cold stirring of dread.

Continuing down the street, they came to a general store, open and lit. They rushed to the counter, which as usual formed the store's fourth wall, opening directly onto the street. No one was there. Incense sticks were smoking in the idol box on the wall above the counter. An open bag of rice stood on the electric scale, and other items on the counter beside it—bars of soap, packages of biscuits, a handful of chillis on a page of newspaper, a box of tea.

"Hello! Hello! Is anyone here?" they shouted into the store in Kannada and English, then turned around and shouted into the street.

An empty liquor store, an empty restaurant, an empty hotel with its adjoining bar, all of them with the same appearance of having been abandoned only a minute before, in terror or in stealth.

Now in full panic, Nada began to run, pulling Zoran with her. They were stumbling down the street hand in hand, fleeing to anywhere, when Nada saw something lying in their path: a body, the body of a dog, the first creature living or dead that they had encountered since waking up some half an hour before. Without hesitating, they ran up and crouched over it.

The dog, a bitch, a typical shorthaired stray, had been disembowelled, apparently within the last minute: blood was gushing from her raggedly torn open belly, and her intestines were strewn over and around her. She was still alive, breathing in shuddering, voiceless whimpers, her grinning mouth chattering as if she were freezing. Nada wept, stroking the dog's ears and head as her life rapidly ebbed away; but Zoran's face showed less horror than resignation, as if what he was seeing merely confirmed something he already knew.

When the shuddering body became still, they remained on their knees for some time, their faces bowed, Nada weeping softly.

"Let's move." Zoran's voice was husky. "Let's get out of here. They're here, *he's* here. They're all around us. Let's move."

They got to their feet and started down the street out of the village, shuffling at first, then walking, then running, hand in hand, until they were again surrounded by fields and uncultivated land, lit by the cool sheen of the stars and gibbous moon. They ran for about an hour, breathing in gasps, down the road that gently snaked through the alternately flat and hilly landscape, devoid of any trace or sound of any living creature.

They passed houses, near and far, lit and unlit, and the distant glow that some village cast on the sky, but Nada no longer had any idea of finding anyone out here, any idea or any wish. All she wanted, all they wanted (she knew it without his saying so, because they said nothing)—all they wanted was to reach the highway: it was unimaginable—even more unimaginable than the unreality they were now experiencing—that the highway would be empty, that there they would not at last find busses, trucks, people, anybody. But the road went on and on, and of the highway there was no sign.

Nada stumbled and fell, taking Zoran down with her, and they tumbled together in the dirt of the road. There they lay, breathing in sobs, and soon actually sobbing, clinging desperately to each other, their faces pressed close. The absence of living things weighed upon her like a presence as they embraced in the middle of the road, knowing that no one was coming, but that someone was watching—one or many, or perhaps the conscious, malevolent land itself. Thus they lay for a long time.

And then Zoran kissed her, once, then again and again, with rising passion. At first she was shocked and confused, turned her face, resisted, but soon began to respond, returning his kisses with equal ardour, like him slipping her hands into his clothes and grasping the beloved flesh that she knew she would soon be parted from, as from her own.

The love Nada made to Zoran was desperate: it was her love for him in what she thought were their final hours or moments of life. But as his embrace shook her ever more violently, she began to feel that he had forgotten fear, and to wonder how his desire could be so untroubled by memory of the nightmare they had lived through that day. She began to feel that Zoran was not really there with her.

And then she remembered the sensation she had had when she awoke with him in front of the temple, that unconscious, imageless bodily memory of a previous lovemaking or violation, of which the one that now possessed her was perhaps only a continuation. The frightening hopelessness that she had seen in Zoran's face as they crouched over the dying dog had completely left him: he was all desire, unambivalent and furious, and she wanted nothing but to be transformed into the same. At moments she looked into his face: he was the picture of ecstasy, head lifted, eyes closed, mouth half-open. Their movements accelerated. They shuddered, cried out, and fell still in each other's arms. After some time they separated, lay side by side on their backs, and fell asleep holding hands.

It was still deep night when Nada was awakened by the sound of Zoran softly weeping. They were still on their backs, with hands joined. She turned her head to the right to look at him, and saw his profile palely lit by moon and stars, streaked with a glistening stream of tears. He remained looking up at the sky, but squeezed her hand when he perceived that she was awake.

"Zoran," she said, "don't be sad. Let's not even be afraid. Whatever is happening to us, we're facing it together. They can kill us, but they can't separate us, they can't come between us."

"He *does* come between us," Zoran replied in a soft, wrenched voice. "It's happened twice. It happened again just now, when we fell asleep here, like it happened when we fell asleep in front of the temple. I see him, I dream of him. Just now again I saw him... making love to you, I saw you making love to him as if he were me."

Dread plunged through Nada like a blade. "Who? Who makes love to me?" she whispered.

49

Zoran's face broke into a sob of agony. "Avinash," he choked. "Avinash."

Darkness rose to claim her, flooded her breast like a freezing underground stream, sounded in her ears like an ocean. She turned her head to look up into the night sky, and for the first time felt despair, which despite her almost certain belief in their imminent death had not arisen in her before, because she had known that that death would be shared.

But now what did they share? How did they possess each other, when Zoran did not even fully possess himself anymore? And who *did* possess him? Was it true what he said? Was he going mad?

But at this moment, at least, he *was* himself, whatever evil may have entered him and perhaps still be lurking somewhere deep within him. The evil seemed to be attached to this place: perhaps they could escape its power by escaping its territory.

Nada got to her feet, fixed her clothes—Zoran evidently made no connection between their unfastened clothes and his dream—and pulled him up by the hand.

She said, "We've got to keep moving, keep trying to reach the highway. Whatever they are, their power must be limited; it may be confined to this place."

They resumed running down the road, ran for what seemed like hours until the sky began to lighten to their left. When the sun broke over the fields and low mountains, they were staggering, exhausted.

Nada saw another village ahead of them, and felt not the least surprise when they found it empty. She knew by now that villages were part of the dream in which they had been trapped, and that their salvation (if there was any hope of that) would only be found if they met some break in the self-mirroring loop of this unreal landscape.

Starving and parched, they went behind the counter of a general store (open and ready, like everything in the village), took dry snack foods and drinks, took fruits and vegetables from the vendors' unattended carts and cloths laid on the ground beside the street, and walked out of the village eating, with the rest in their knapsacks.

The food and drink gave Nada a new fund of energy for a few more hours as they walked through the evacuated countryside. But by the time the sun was over their heads, she was again heavy with exhaustion, and the shade of roadside trees beckoned irresistibly.

"But we can't both sleep at once," said Zoran nervously. "We'll take turns."

They turned off the road and lay down in the grass under a thick-trunked tree whose broad shade could be counted on to protect them from the sun for hours to come.

"I'm not ready to sleep yet," said Zoran, sitting up against the trunk.

Nada lay down with her head in his lap, and looked up into his exhausted, hopeless face, ravaged within the cycle of a day by terror, jealousy, guilt, paranoia.

Closing her eyes, she instantly drifted off, but resisted deep sleep, remained anchored to consciousness of the beautiful hot day, the breeze, the breathing foliage above them, Zoran's hands stilly caressing her face, his own face looking defeated but infused with the deep unshakable love that knows that the final hours have come. Eventually she began to sink away, and then she began to feel a third presence, another awareness, invisible but close, like a threatening whisper mingled with the tree's breath or deep within her own mind.

She felt Zoran shaking her awake.

"Nada, I'm sinking. Wake up. Watch me. I'm so sorry."

She sat up slowly, caressed his face—he had already nearly drifted off—took his place against the tree trunk as he laid his head in her lap. She looked towards the west, where the sun would touch the distant mountains within about two hours. She didn't know how long she had slept, but she was sufficiently revived that she didn't feel herself to be in danger of falling asleep again soon. She took occasional chugs from a bottle of cola to fortify her wakefulness.

Nightfall held no special terror for her, since whatever was stalking them was evidently no more dangerous by night than by day. She felt that it would soon reveal itself again—as three men, as one, as someone or something else entirely—and that it would probably kill them this time, instantaneously and brutally, like it had killed the dog, the only example they had witnessed of what it was capable of—besides the disappearance of all living things.

She was resigned to this end, mostly, and deeply worn out and defeated, but her slim belief in the possibility of escape was still stronger than despair, and this is what kept her going. They were young, they were in love, they had planned their life together until old age. Behind the weariness and defeat that almost made her want to stop and wait for their imminent death, there still burned a flame of blinding indignation at this stranger who had come out of nowhere and invaded their life, insinuated himself into the sacred space between them which was theirs alone, and into their very bodies, contaminating the purity of their intimacy and devotion. They *would* get away, and if this miracle were achieved, she would defy fate even further: she would hunt their tormentor down and kill him.

She sat awake with these thoughts as she watched the sun sink, and just minutes before it touched the distant mountains (was there anything left alive in all that vast distance?), Zoran awoke.

He turned onto his back so that he was looking up into Nada's face, and she caressed his as she watched the sun sink into the earth. She now perceived that the road they had been walking led more or less towards the south.

"The highway will be that way, towards the sunset," she said. "Any road we find going that way, we have to take."

Zoran sat up, then they stood up and embraced, holding each other tight for a long time as the darkness thickened. And then they set off on the same southward-leading road through blackness punctuated by a few rare lights of houses near and far. The gibbous moon was already high, cold small and white, and the winter sky, almost untouched by earthly light, was infinitely deep with stars.

They walked briskly, sometimes hand in hand, their breath clouding before their faces. After some hours, on the left-hand side of the road ahead of them a temple appeared, fully lit as if for a public ritual. As they neared it, they slowed, as if drawn by fascination, and approached the door, from which a slab of light fell across the road.

As they stood and looked within, Nada saw an idol unlike any she had seen before in a temple's place of honour, though she had seen others like it in peripheral positions—at doorways and on pillars and walls—in the precincts of other temples. It was a *rakshasa,* a demon, fanged and grinning, wide-eyed and sharp-eared, with radiating locks. It was crouched on its haunches, holding out its empty hands as if it were waiting to receive some gift. Its eyes were painted white, its mouth smeared with blood and globs of flesh. A heavy garland of roses hung around its neck, and rose petals were strewn about its feet. Small lit earthen lamps covered the floor around it. The walls were everywhere streaked with handprints of blood flecked with flesh, as if people had been locked in the temple's tiny space and had gone mad trying to claw their way out.

They were drawn towards the temple's doorway. There was a noise from behind them, a voice.

Nada turned. It was the friendly whimpering of a dog that was standing in the road staring at them, wagging its tail uncertainly. She took a step towards it, and almost swooned as it dawned on her that this was the bitch they had seen die in the village the night before. A surge of terror flooded her. She whirled round.

Zoran was lying prostrate before the idol on the rose petal-sprinkled floor. Blood was gushing from his severed neck, flooding the floor, spraying the idol and the walls. His head rested in the *rakshasa's* hands, facing away from her.

Nada walked slowly forward, tears streaming down her face, which registered no fear, no shock, only love robbed of all hope. She approached the idol, crouched in the still flowing blood, gently took the head in her hands, slowly lifted its tremendous weight from the demon's claws. She began to turn it towards her. Even before its living red eye met hers, even before she saw its slightly smiling mouth and lupine fangs, she knew it was not Zoran. It was the man in front of the temple. And he was Avinash.

Nada stood up, and the head thudded to the concrete floor. She began to scream, scream with every shuddering breath. She ran, blindly, stumbling, her arms flailing, ran and ran with no sense of direction or time, until there were sounds and lights somewhere, and solid pavement under her feet, the roar of engines, the howling of braking tires, the piercing melody of a truck's horn, the great blinding multicoloured wall of a truck suddenly in front of her, the voices of men shouting and speaking in Kannada as she lay on her back on the road, screaming and screaming.

The last trace of daylight was fading as Nada walked down Usha Road towards *Yadnya.* After the Institute had closed at five-thirty, she and Shyamala had sat talking on a bench outside the library until seven, and had then come to Usha Road and eaten at Sahadev, one of Nada's favourite restaurants. Shyamala had then gone back to her scooter at the Institute, and Nada had begun to walk the short remaining distance to *Yadnya.* She had just reached the house's low stone wall when she heard a voice from behind her.

"Professor Marjanovic?"

She turned, and felt a bolt of ice go through her as she saw Avinash standing before her on the footpath, but immediately doubted her judgement: this man looked physically exactly like Avinash, but everything else—his clothes, his aura, the look in his eyes—was different.

He was dressed in the attire of the traditional Karnataka Brahmin, with sacred thread, loincloth, and head shaved except for a long topknot, and wore on his left ring finger a simple silver ring. And the hate and mockery, the seething menace that radiated from Avinash, were not here; instead, this man's face registered mildness and reserve, and at the moment, hesitancy.

He did not move towards her, evidently aware of the process going on in her mind. After a pause, he continued: "I am Amruteshvar. Amruteshvar Chandrashekhar. In a sense, we already know each other.

imām amṛtajijñāsāṃ kṛtavān amṛteśvaraḥ
rakṣaṇāya ca lokasya vetālaśamanāya ca

Nada almost reeled when she heard him speak this verse from the first chapter of the *Amrutajijnasa* in which the book's author identifies himself: "Amruteshvara wrote this *Amrutajijnasa* to protect the world and lay the *vetala* to rest."

She was stunned, but also began to feel reassured: she was almost certain that Avinash would not even have been able to utter the words of Amruteshvar, whose very name meant "master of the undead." Indeed, one of the strange things about Avinash's performance at the conference in Zagreb was that he had never once quoted the words, or even the name, of the text with which he seemed somehow to be so intimately familiar, despite presumably never having even seen it himself.

Nada approached him. By now she felt no need to put challenge in her voice: she didn't know *how* this could be Amruteshvar, but she was satisfied that, somehow, it was. Wasn't everything surrounding this book impossible anyway?

"I'm sure you must know that Dr. Kshirasagar has died, more than a week ago," she said. "You must also know that he and I were friends for many years. But he certainly never mentioned that he had met you... and... how would that have been possible, anyway? How *is* this possible?" she asked, now standing directly in front of him, amazed, studying this face that was indeed that of her ancient foe in every way except for the character that invested it.

The absolute difference of this man's aura allowed her to realize, for the first time, the beauty of this face, the depth of humanity that its lineaments were capable of communicating. And there was some kind of *relief* in this, as if she were grateful for the *permission* to find something positive, something good, in this image that had pursued her day and night for half a lifetime.

"Yes, I knew Dr. Kshirasagar—better than he realized, better than he knew me. He never really met *me,* though we met again and again. Professor Marjanovic—Nada?— I'm just going to have to ask you to trust me. I'm Avinash Chandrashekhar's brother, but I am his enemy—or more precisely, I am the enemy of what he has become. I have other very strange things to tell you—but after all they're no stranger than anything in the *Amrutajijnasa,* or in your own history with that book. You have personally experienced many of the impossible things it describes; now you only have to accept that *all* of those things are true."

His voice was exactly like Avinash's, with the same difference that distinguished his face from that of his twin: it sounded good, not evil; it was kind, open, unasserting, not hostile, guarded, mocking.

"May I come inside?" he said. "We're going to begin to attract attention here."

Nada hesitated. "*I* trust you," she said; "I'm already putting things together. But ... you know Kamala, of course, Dr. Kshirasagar's wife. She'll be terrified if she sees you. I wouldn't be surprised if she died on the spot of a heart attack."

"I understand," said Amruteshvar. "I'll take care of that. But we're going to have to go in sooner or later, and I'm going to need to keep coming back. You need my help—with the book, with everything. Tell her you've met an old acquaintance of Dr. Kshirasagar, a *friend*."

Nada thought, then nodded.

"Come, then," she said, turning and walking towards the gap in the wall.

Amruteshvar followed. Nada took a key from her pocket, then turned to him and said, "Let me go in first and let her know you're with me."

She unlocked the door and went in, while he sat on the edge of the concrete barrier surrounding the ancient *ashoka* tree in the front yard.

Passing through the front porch and the second door, Nada entered the hall, where she found Kamala lying on her pallet in the darkness. She sat up when she heard Nada come in, and Nada went over and sat on the edge of the pallet.

"*Maushi*," she said in Marathi, the language in which she always talked with her, using the respectful but affectionate title—"auntie"—with which one normally addresses an older woman. "I've met someone who can

59

give me important help with finishing Dr. Kshirasagar's work. He was an old acquaintance of the doctor, and he's our friend. His name is Amruteshshvar. He's waiting outside. May he come in?"

Kamala hesitated, perhaps struck by the name, so long familiar to her from the discussions in this house. Then she nodded and said, "Yes, bring him in."

Nada went back out into the front yard, and was about to speak to Amruteshvar when she stopped.

As he turned his face to her, she saw that it had changed: he still looked essentially like Avinash, but now more like a fraternal than an identical twin.

Kamarupi, she thought, *changing form at will*.

He rose and came inside with her.

When they came into the hall, Amruteshvar joined his hands in *namaskar* to Kamala, and said in perfect Marathi, "Mrs. Kshirasagar, I met your husband many times over the years. I knew him—better than he knew me—and I know the *Amrutajijnasa* very well. I know Nada too, though we have only now met in person for the first time. I've come to help her finish Dr. Kshirasagar's work—now more than ever, it's important to finish this work. So I hope you won't mind having me in your house. I will not need to *live* here, but I will need to work here with Nada and Shyamala."

Kamala was looking at him intently, trying to remember, perhaps, where she might have seen this face before, as Nada suspected.

"Of course you can be here," she replied at last. "Any

friend of my husband is forever welcome in his house." She rose and said, "Would you like tea and something to eat?"

"No thank you," he replied, "I'd rather get right to work—and since the manuscript and Dr. Kshirasagar's commentary still haven't been brought back here from the Institute, tonight that work will consist of *talking* about work."

Not in the least bit surprised that Amruteshvar knew everything, Nada said: "Shyamala and I were going to bring the manuscript straight here in a rickshaw tomorrow. I didn't want to be walking the streets with it. Now that you're here we can do it even more safely. For now, let's go to the study upstairs—I'm sure you already know the way."

She turned to Kamala. "Are you all right down here on your own, *Maushi?* Obviously you can join us if you want—like in the old days." Kamala smiled sadly and shook her head, and Nada turned and opened the door to the stairs.

The study and Nada's bedroom were the only rooms on the small house's second floor. The study's south and west sides had large windows which looked out onto the small yard with its two large trees, an *ashoka* and a mango tree. Under the larger of the two windows stood a small pallet like the one Kamala slept on in the living room downstairs. The other two walls were covered by bookshelves, and the floor space on that side was dominated by a large wooden desk, on which there stood a short row of books and a table lamp.

Nada turned the heavy wooden chair that stood at the desk, and gestured to Amruteshvar to sit down on its twin a few feet away.

"Have you ever actually been in here before," she asked in English when they were both seated, "or do you know the place in some other way?"

"I have been here several times," Amruteshvar answered, "but not in the form in which you see me now. Dr. Kshirasagar never saw me like this, though this—or rather, the way I appeared to you before I entered the house—is my true form. He met various experts in *vetalashastra* over the years, here at the Institute and elsewhere. I was those experts. It was at my suggestion that Dr. Kashyap of Mysore gave Kshirasagar the *Amrutajijnasa.* I have had an intense interest in this book for a very long time. No one knows this book better than I do, because I wrote it; but there are still a few... problems with the text that I actually can't resolve myself, for which I need the help of others."

Nada appeared calm as she heard all this. She was burning with excitement, but it was the excitement of hearing confirmed what she had been blindly guessing at for years. And even though it was all being revealed in such an unreal way, and with so many details that she could never have imagined, the gratification and relief that came from finally knowing far outweighed any dread that she might have felt at learning that such terrible things were, after all, true.

"Well, having you here will certainly make our work

a lot quicker," she said. "For example, since you wrote it, you can immediately clear up what has always been the text's big mystery for us: what are the missing words of this verse's third quarter?

na śastreṇa na śāstreṇa nihantuṃ śakyate 'mṛtaḥ

And this isn't just a textual problem, of course: once we know this, we know how to kill the *vetala*—or is it *give him peace* rather than *kill?* You tell me."

"I can help with a lot of things," Amruteshvar replied, "but there are a few things that I can't tell you, things that won't be valid or efficacious unless you find them out for yourself. And this is one of them. And of course that's why the text is mutilated at this point and only at this point: the efficacy of the whole *Amrutajijnasa* rests on these eight syllables. Without them, it's just a lot of interesting information; with them, it's an instrument of liberation for both the *vetala* and his victims."

"Can you at least tell me how the text was mutilated, and who did it?" asked Nada.

"It was Avinash, of course," said Amruteshvar, "but long ago, and in a different form. He would have destroyed the whole book, if he could have, but it was almost impossible for him to be in its presence at all, so he focused all his hate and fear on this most critical point."

"And of course you remember exactly what the missing words are," said Nada.

"Obviously."

"And you can't tell me because... if you did, they wouldn't work, *for me,* and all the information in the *Amrutajijnasa* would become impotent in my hands."

"That's right," said Amruteshvar, smiling with a touch of what might have been compassion. "But you can do it, you can figure out what the missing words are. I've always known that, or I wouldn't be here, and would never even have inspired Dr. Kashyap to give the book to Dr. Kshirasagar in the first place. I've always had faith in you people, I've always known that you were the ones who would finally be able to realize the purpose of my book—and free my brother."

They sat in silence for a moment. Then Nada said: "It's been seven hundred years since you wrote the *Amrutajijnasa.* In it, you say at one point:

vetālo naram āviśya saṃniṣṭhāyā 'ntarātmani
jātaṃ jātaṃ tam anveti yāvan no 'paiti rakṣitā

Which I think must mean: 'After the *vetala* has entered a man and established himself in his inmost soul, he follows him through birth after birth, until his saviour appears.' So how many times has Avinash been reborn since then? And you're twins. Have you always been twins? Have you been reborn together again and again over the centuries, or is this the first time for one or both of you?"

"We've been reborn again and again, together, and always in the same roles—you must have noticed that Avinash's name means 'undying.' But it wasn't until this

64

birth that we fully remembered, and realized what was going on. Seven hundred years ago we were what we are now: Brahmins born into a family of scholars, twins born to walk the same path, but destined to be separated by an alien spirit that had entered one of us and inspired him with evil. You know how to think about this, because I talk about it repeatedly, in terms of the story of King Nala and Damayanti in the *Mahabharata*:

> *kalir nalaṃ yathā' viṣṭo vijahāra mano' lpaśaḥ*
> *vetālasyā' pi sa tathā haraty ātmānam ātmanaḥ*

As Kali entered Nala and took away his mind bit by bit, so does he carry the *vetala's* self away from himself.

When my brother was first possessed, I had the means to understand what had happened; I wrote the *Amrutajijnasa* in order to try to understand, and to free him. In the births between that one and this present one, we have always been brothers, and we have always acted out the same drama of alienation, but we didn't remember the birth in which it had begun. Once we were rag pickers, once we were farmers, once we were merchants, once we were ministers of a king. Sometimes we were even animals. Always it was the same: we would begin as friends, both of us on the same side; but then a spirit of evil would arise in him and draw him away, rivalry would undermine our brotherhood. Because once the *vetala* entered him, it never left him, birth after birth; it was only ever a matter of time before it awoke and asserted itself."

"But I still don't understand why you need anybody's help," said Nada. "Why all this time, why so many births? Why this roundabout way, with you writing a book and then looking for someone to implement its teaching? Why didn't you write the book, learn what you needed to know, and then carry it out yourself seven hundred years ago?"

"That's a good question," replied Amruteshvar. "That was the original plan, and I did almost accomplish it. I was certainly determined and energetic enough. But I lacked one thing." He sighed. "The *vetala's* victim can only be freed by someone who loves him. And in the end it turned out that I just didn't love him enough."

"Then why on earth have you come to me?" asked Nada, her voice trembling with controlled rage, her eyes shining.

Amruteshvar looked at her sadly, and did not say a word.

Nada found herself in the woods on Vetal Tekadi, Vampire Hill. It was night, and no one else was there, but she felt that she was looking for someone, or that someone was looking for her, as she stumbled along the unlit path, with the city's lights glowing from beyond the dense hillside foliage, and immediately below, the few dim lights of the Institute.

The usual sounds were missing: there was no humming of crickets, no cries of the *kokil,* the Indian cuckoo. A thick, murky silence seemed to smother everything. Nada was naked, and vaguely concerned that this might become a problem if she happened to meet anyone, but still she stumbled on, until she came to the temple of the *vetalaraja,* the King of Vampires, at the point where the path turned sharply at the edge of the hill.

A dog lay in the path before the temple, alertly watching her, and as she approached she saw a man sitting on the bench in front. It was Avinash: even though he was dressed in the traditional costume that Amruteshvar wore, she knew that it was Avinash, because she was aware that *she* had become Amruteshvar, while at the same time somehow still being herself, still troubled by her nudity.

He watched her as she approached. His face was free of the menace and mockery with which she had always seen it invested. She stood before him. His eyes were pleading, desperate. He seemed to be speaking in English, but she couldn't make out the words, even though she knew what he was saying: *Help me, brother. Save me. Forgive me.*

She noticed that the dog was lying on the ground behind the bench, looking elsewhere, and realized that it was the bitch they had seen die in the village twenty-five years before.

She turned to the temple, an open, wall-less structure that she had many times come to see, where people sacrificed goats and chickens to the idol of the *vetalaraja*. The idol, a shapeless painted stone, was missing, and in its place stood the rose-garlanded *rakshasa* before which Zoran had died.

In front of it, a sari-clad woman's body hung from the roof by a knotted cloth. Nada walked across the concrete floor, thick with clotted blood and fragments of flesh, and looked up into her face. It was a beautiful face, fair and narrow, calm as if in sleep, with slightly opened mouth and vacant, frozen eyes. Nada contemplated her with mild wonder, and felt a strangely detached pity for her, and behind this, a vague sense, touched with dread, that she ought to know who this woman was.

She looked beyond the body and saw Avinash standing at the far end of the temple floor. He was weeping, again speaking words that Nada could not make out but which she understood: *Forgive me, forgive me.* She looked past Avinash and saw that it was now Amruteshvar who was sitting on the bench, indistinguishable from his brother in all but his familiar expression of resigned, knowing sadness.

She again looked up at the woman's face, and realized that it was her own, felt hands of darkness rising to claim her, felt herself being propelled forcefully upward as if to the surface of water. She jolted awake, staring at the ceiling of her room in *Yadnya,* her heart pounding.

She lay thus for some minutes as her heartbeat slowed and she oriented herself to the current facts of her waking reality, which took some effort, since they were scarcely less bizarre than the dream she had just awakened from.

It had not yet begun to dawn. The mournful, exuberant cries of *kokils* cut through the silence near and far. The room glowed faintly with moonlight. Cool air poured through the open window. Nada was lying naked on her back under the small bed's mosquito net.

She thought of her meeting with Amruteshvar, and the task of the coming day. He had declined to stay the night at *Yadnya,* and had not said where he was going. They had agreed to meet at the Institute in the morning, and bring the manuscript to the house in an autorickshaw—despite his reservations: it would be safer to hire a car, or even to walk, he had said, but she had insisted that there would really be no danger if they travelled in her favourite vehicle, and he had yielded to her.

She shifted onto her side and reviewed last night's

conversation. What Amruteshvar had told her had been more than enough to take in at one sitting, but now that she had put it all together she was thinking of the gaps she would need him to fill.

How had Avinash become a *vetala* in the first place? Why had he been entered and possessed by this malevolent spirit? That such a spirit should be able to retain possession of his victim through multiple incarnations was novel and perplexing, but somehow less mysterious than whatever mechanism of karma continued to bind the unpossessed Amruteshvar to his brother.

And where did Amruteshvar get the supernatural powers he evidently had if he was not himself a *vetala?* And most importantly... *why her?*

She would have to ask him about all this while they worked here together on the text. And yet of course, as he had told her, not all of that work could be done by both of them together: the most important part of it, the cracking of the text's code, she would have to do alone, because... Amruteshvar didn't love his brother enough. Whereas *she...?*

The sky had grown pale with the first degree of dawn, and the *kokils'* shouts, cycling from far to near, were growing more frequent. Nada began to drift off again.

It was her lifelong habit, while living on her own, to rise and begin working at the *brahmamuhurta,* the holy hour before dawn, but without the text here, and with the Institute's opening time still hours away, there was no strong reason for her to get up now, and besides, the night before she had stayed up well beyond her usual bedtime talking with Amruteshvar.

Her thoughts began to be coloured by the hallucinatory logic of dream. As she thought of how she would be meeting Amruteshvar at the Institute within a few hours, she saw him, or more precisely felt him, standing in the back yard under the mango tree, while another presence appeared at her window: a huge *vatavaghul,* a fruit bat, clinging upside down to the window's bars and staring at her nakedness with red eyes. Just before she sank into oblivion in the pale glow of dawn, she saw that a second bat had joined the first and clung to him from behind, gripping him by the neck with lupine fangs as they both stared at her body on the bed.

Hours later, in the manuscriptorium, Nada lifted the red cloth-bound manuscript from the iron cabinet as Ekbote, Bhave, Shyamala, and Amruteshvar stood by.

"I'm glad we're getting this done," she said, gently putting the bundle, still with the rosary, into a heavy metal carrying box that stood waiting on a small writing desk nearby, and closing and padlocking the lid.

She turned to them. "Shyamala, we'll see you at *Yadnya* later today, right?"

Shyamala nodded.

"OK, let's find a rickshaw," said Nada, effortfully picking up the box and moving towards the Institute's main entrance while Bhave spoke to a groundskeeper, who went off to hail one. "Yes, I know," she said, smiling a little apologetically at Amruteshvar, who clearly intended her to see his expression of silent resignation. "But you know I simply cannot stand riding in hired cars, like some self-styled VIP. It's just not me. And anyway, what could happen? I have you with me." He looked down, apparently less than reassured, but she barely noticed: having known him for less than a day, her confidence in him was already unshakable.

"It's been a pleasure to meet you," said Bhave to Amruteshvar as they all walked through the main hall. "I hope to see you here at the Institute from time to time while you're in Pune."

"Oh, you definitely will," he replied. "It's been a while since I was last here, and with the way the neighbourhood has changed, I don't foresee that there are going to be many places between here and *Yadnya* that will draw me in."

Nada had introduced Amruteshvar as Avinash's brother and another expert in *vetalashastra,* and left it at that, and Bhave had accepted this, being sufficiently familiar, probably, with the weird atmosphere of secrecy and anxiety that surrounded this book that she knew better than to ask unnecessary questions. Amruteshvar had again softened his likeness to his brother, so that he now looked like a fraternal rather than an identical twin, as he had when he had entered *Yadnya.*

When they came out of the Institute's main entrance, the groundskeeper was standing there with the auto-rickshaw, and Nada and Amruteshvar got in.

"*Acireṇa,*" said Nada to Shyamala, smiling—Sanskrit

for *in a bit*—then gave the rickshaw driver directions in Marathi, and they set off down the sun-baked drive that led to Malati Road.

As they paused on the edge of the busy street waiting to cross it and drive down Tilak Institute Road, Nada glimpsed the driver's eye looking at her in the small circular rear-view mirror. It was blazing with hate and fury, and its iris was red.

"Amruteshvar!" she shouted. "Get out! It's him!"

The rickshaw lurched into motion, turning violently to the left onto Malati Road and weaving through the thick traffic of scooters, motorcycles, cars, and other rickshaws as Nada and Amruteshvar were hurled from side to side against each other, Nada protectively hunching over the metal box in her lap.

Amruteshvar struggled to find a handhold, his face unsurprised and determined. Just as he succeeded in grasping one of the metal bars in front of him, they reached the point where the road turned sharply to the left, skirting the Institute's large grounds. Amruteshvar lost his hold and was almost thrown from the right door, hitting his head on its metal frame, as Nada, fiercely embracing the box, crashed into his side.

Oncoming vehicles loomed before them again and again as the rickshaw dodged through traffic moving in both directions. Amruteshvar had again gripped the bar in front of him with both hands and was evidently waiting for an instant when he could release a hand and lunge at the driver. He hissed something in a strange Kannada that

Nada was not able to follow, and the driver shot a backward glance at him over his right shoulder. His face was unrecognizable, a stranger's, flabby, middle-aged, and unshaven—the real driver whose body, like his vehicle, had been hijacked by the *vetala* for his own purposes—but the hate that wrenched that face was Avinash's, as were the red eyes and the fangs in its snarling mouth.

He snapped his gaze back towards the road, where a bus was towering before them like a moving wall. Its horn shook the air as it attempted to avoid a collision by veering to its left, but the rickshaw driver now drove straight for the bus.

Amruteshvar threw his arms around Nada and hurled himself forward, bearing her out of the left door at the instant of impact. They tumbled onto the road, Amruteshvar still wrapped around her, as the bus ploughed into the rickshaw with a glassy thud, its right wheels missing them by inches, and hurtled past them, dragging the crumpled vehicle which had turned onto its side and lodged under the bus's fender, projecting from it on the right. Pinned beneath the wrecked rickshaw, the driver's body trailed behind it, his arms dragging, his face leaving a path of gore on the pavement. The bus struck aside cars, motorcycles, and scooters as it veered off the road and crashed into the rocky face of a low hill on the margin of the Institute's land.

Amruteshvar and Nada lay in the middle of the road, with vehicles flying towards and past them in both directions, Nada still desperately clutching the metal box to her chest. Amruteshvar sprang to his feet, grasping Nada by the arm. Vehicles continued to dart around them, horns sounding and tires screaming. Veering to avoid them, a car struck Amruteshvar's side with a dull metallic sound of impact and bounced aside as if it had struck another car as Amruteshvar moved towards the roadside, pulling Nada with him. For just an instant, it occurred to Nada that not only had she survived, but she was completely unscathed, and not only was she unscathed, but she had never lost hold of the box.

When they were off the road, Nada heard what sounded like a series of explosions. She looked towards the bus some twenty feet away, and saw body after body bursting through the windows and tumbling lifeless onto the ground. A figure was moving around inside.

Amruteshvar began to run towards the bus. Nada stood watching him, fiercely embracing the box, still focussed on their mission, thinking of how they could get away as quickly as possible and get the manuscript safely to *Yadnya*.

She called after him: "Amruteshvar! The manuscript! We... we have to get out of here!"

Without stopping or looking back, he shouted: "People are going to die—because of *us*."

She felt a nauseating wave of shame. Yes, it was true. Because of *her*. She ran after him, slowed by her burden, which she awkwardly continued to press against her chest with both arms.

Passengers' crumpled, bloody bodies lay on the rocky

ground to the vehicle's right and rear where they had fallen after being hurled through the glass; on the other side, they continued to hurtle through the windows. Except for the explosive sound of breaking glass, a dreadful silence invested the scene, and as she approached, Nada understood its cause: no one who had survived such brutal injuries could have had the strength even to groan, and she doubted that many had survived.

Nada looked up and saw that the figure inside was Avinash, recognizably himself this time, but dressed in the uniform of the bus driver and with massive wounds on his head and shoulder. He looked straight at her through one of the glassless windows, his red eyes blazing.

Before she could react, she perceived a sudden movement to her right, and looked to see Amruteshvar running and leaping over bodies to reach the rear door, where a dark young girl in a blood-soaked sari lay crumpled on the bottom step, her trembling hands weakly groping at nothing. He stooped over her, caressing her head with both hands and intently looking her over, then tenderly lifted her and laid her on the ground between two other bodies.

Then he turned, his own face now suffused with a cold fury that made it indistinguishable from his brother's, lunged into the doorway and up the stairs, and hurled himself on Avinash, who received him grinning and open-armed. The impact shook the whole bus, lifting it momentarily off the ground with a shower of glass from the shattered windows.

Avinash was knocked off his feet and borne backwards the length of the bus and out the gaping front window, where both brothers slammed against the rock and fell out of sight. In the next instant the bus kicked backwards and flew off the ground, then landed with a shuddering crash only a few feet away from Nada, revealing Amruteshvar and Avinash standing face to face in combat stance.

Avinash leapt on his brother like a tiger, and the two tumbled onto the ground, struggling with each other. Avinash got a grip on his brother's throat and wrestled him onto his back. As he sat on Amruteshvar's chest, pinning his shoulders to the ground, Avinash's face was so transformed by a grin of hate that he ceased to resemble himself. His mouth grew enormous, every tooth became a spearlike fang. Nada was shaken by sympathetic horror as she saw him dart his head forward like a snake striking; with his now vast maw he engulfed Amruteshvar's whole face in a ring of teeth and ripped it away, leaving a featureless mass of bloody flesh. Amruteshvar's body went limp.

Nada screamed, "Amruteshvar! Oh my god! Oh my god!"

Still hunched over his brother, Avinash snapped his head round and looked at Nada. Crimson chunks and threads dripped from his fangs. Amruteshvar's death, and the certain imminence of her own, inspired Nada with the defiance of despair. She felt her features settle into a look of cool determination as she hugged the metal box to her chest with both arms, ready to go down fighting with all her strength.

Turning back to his brother, Avinash plunged huge bladelike claws into his abdomen, and drew them back steaming with gore. Then he leapt to his feet, turned to face Nada, and with a single bound crossed the twenty feet of space that separated them, landing immediately in front of her.

With his huge demonic face an inch away from hers, he released a searing scream that blew Nada off her feet. She was thrown backwards, dropping the box, and tumbled breathlessly to the ground some distance away.

Avinash seized the box with dripping claws, and roared in agony as his and his brother's flesh sizzled and smoked on contact with the metal. He quickly lifted the box and hurled it through the bus's smashed rear window, then leapt to its front door and scrambled up the steps and into the driver's seat. The engine groaned to life and the bus lurched backwards, heading straight for Nada, who only just managed to reorient herself and roll out of the way the instant before the wheels would have crushed her.

Shuddering and crashing, bouncing crazily up and down, the bus continued to hurtle backwards up the rocky slope and towards the road, now lined with a huge throng of vehicles and gawking people who began to scatter as it neared.

Without pausing to reflect on the miracle of her survival, again focused on the day's original mission, Nada scrambled to her feet and ran towards the bus as it thundered onto the road, smashing vehicles and crushing people under its rear wheels. As it pounded to a stop she reached its rear door, and grabbing the handbar, yanked herself onto the bottom step just before the bus leapt forward, ploughing into everything in its path and taking off down Malati Road.

Clutching the back of the last seat with both hands, Nada managed to slowly climb the steps of the rear entrance as the bus swayed wildly back and forth, weaving through traffic. Embracing the last pole in the aisle, fighting to stay on her feet, she looked forward and saw Avinash in the driver's seat and the box on the floor of the aisle two or three rows behind him. A dead man slumped in one seat on the left with his head hanging out of the smashed window, the glass mangling the flesh of his neck. Farther ahead on the other side, a woman lay on her back, pinned in place by her sari, which had caught on the seat's back; vacant eyes staring, her head lolled into the aisle at a sickeningly unnatural angle, jerking up and down as the bus crashed along the road. With effort, Nada mastered the turmoil of guilt and pity that threatened to cloud her mind, and steeled herself for her task.

Grasping the backs of the seats on both sides, straddling the aisle, she slowly made her way forward, almost thrown off her feet at every step. Looking up, she saw Avinash's red eyes glaring at her in the rear-view mirror. The bus twisted to the left with a deafening screech of tires. The force of the turn ripped the man's corpse from the window and hurled it like a doll against the opposite seats. Nada clenched her eyes shut with the effort of holding on.

Within moments, she opened them again, alarmed:

the bus was now moving uphill on a trafficless road, and she realized that this was the narrow side-road to the top of Vetal Tekadi.

Of course: Avinash couldn't bear to touch the manuscript himself, so he was going to drive the bus off the cliff at the end of the road, and the fireball that would consume it at the foot of the hill would destroy both the book and its protector—or only its protector, but her death would neutralize whatever potential danger the book posed to him, perhaps forever.

As the bus careened up the hill, step by slow step Nada neared the box at the head of the aisle, cringing as she passed the dead woman with her flopping head and vacant eyes.

Now she could see Avinash's whole face in the rearview mirror, his eyes that watched her difficult progress with burning hate; the face was again recognizably his, though the blood caked about the fanged, gnashing mouth recorded the hideous change that had transformed it in the moment when he had destroyed his brother.

Amruteshvar! Gone! And it was her fault!

Now it was between Nada and the monster, she alone had this one last chance to destroy the *vetala* and free the man. A final lurching step, and her foot touched the box; letting go of the seats on both sides, she pounced on it, gripping it with both hands, crouching over it with maternal protectiveness.

Avinash was now just ahead of her to her right, almost within reach. Snarling like an animal, he turned again and again to glare at her over his shoulder, and began to grasp at her with his left hand. She ducked her head and dragged the heavy box back a bit, then fumbled in her pocket for the key, which she had chained to her belt for the anticipated short rickshaw journey back to *Yadnya*.

After several wide misses, she succeeded in inserting it into the keyhole and unlocking the box, then seized the red bundle inside. Even in this nightmare, when the only way to save her life was to use the manuscript as a weapon, it was only with great difficulty that she managed to overcome her philologist's instinct to keep it protected.

Bracing herself on her knees, holding it in front of her with both hands, she lunged forward and thrust it against Avinash's wounded and exposed left shoulder. He screamed inhumanly as his flesh sizzled and smoked at the touch of the red cloth.

Nada leaned against him with all her weight. He turned. Their faces were inches apart. In his red eyes she saw hate, desperation, pleading, fear, the struggle between the original man and an alien evil that had deeply corrupted but still not completely vanquished him.

A tremendous pity filled her, pity and resolution, and she leaned into him even harder. He screamed again and again as the red cloth burned into his lacerated flesh with a sizzling sound, sending up a foul smoke.

Suddenly, Nada could no longer see the road through the front window, only a panorama of the suburbs and surrounding countryside far below. At a point where the road turned sharply upwards and to the left, the bus had shot straight off the cliff, and now seemed to Nada to be suspended in space and time. The city's vastness filled the window from horizon to horizon.

Avinash was still facing her. The evil had gone out of his face, leaving only fear and desperation, now mingled with recognition and gratitude. Even his eyes had turned from red to brown.

This was the man himself, the real Avinash, whoever he had been before being invaded and corrupted by the monster he now was. They stood frozen, face to face, Nada pressing the book into his shoulder, as the bus imperceptibly began its descent to the ground far below. With the sluggish slowness of dream, the horizon crept upwards towards the top of the window and slipped out of sight.

They were tipping forward and falling. The window now looked down on a grid of streets and houses that faded out where the rocks and trees of the hillside began. Alarm began to nag at the edge of her attention. Still pressing the book against Avinash's shoulder, she detached her gaze from his and turned it towards the rising menace of the ground while he continued to stare at her with an expression that had become serene and loving. She felt her guts wrenched by the conflicting claims of gravity and the velocity of their fall. Her eyes and mouth slowly widened into a scream.

She felt a new element move into the scene of imminent impact framed by the window, a huge dark form that swooped from just above the bus's roof, then rose and disappeared into the bus itself, where she felt it hovering behind her head, a somehow benevolent presence.

Now staring at whatever was behind Nada, Avinash's face had moved through surprise to rage. The ground accelerated to meet them with an almost audible tremendousness. By now it was clear where the impact would occur. They were on a level with the top floors of two apartment towers, moving towards a spot on the street between them, close to where it ended in rocks and vegetation at the foot of the hill. She could see the upper branches of a great tree stretching like grasping fingers into the bus's glassless front window. Beneath the tree were parked two cars. They would come down on the front of one and the rear of the other. Nada felt herself enfolded in a warm darkness that drew her, still clutching the manuscript, gently back from Avinash and into itself. The last thing she saw was Avinash's face, again a red-eyed mask of pure demonic fury and hate, at the moment when the window frame met the two cars with a distant drawn-out roar of twisting metal and bursting glass.

By now everything seemed distant to Nada as she felt herself moving upwards in the embrace of a protecting darkness. An enormous jolt of thunder and heat touched her gently from afar as she was drawn into fearless sleep. She began to dream of all that had just happened—getting the manuscript at the Institute, the rickshaw ride, the crash, the bus ride—saw it all through a lens of calm, happy wonder which stripped even Avinash of his menace, and made him one of them, a fellow-sufferer, a brother—even, conceivably, a friend and lover, in another life.

She began to see them all in that other life, too, in flashes interspersed among the scenes of the chase: Nada (but she looked like someone else) walking close to Avinash in the forest. Nada and Avinash sitting on the ground in front of an old-fashioned village house eating a meal with Amruteshvar, all of them dressed in the quietly splendid garments of long ago. Avinash and Amruteshvar facing each other, frowning and angry. Nada and Avinash sitting side by side on a rock in the forest, him reaching out and touching her chin as she looked down and aside, smiling with embarrassment and hidden love.

Then the past was gone, and she again saw the street at the foot of Vetal Tekadi, now scattered with flaming debris around the remains of the bus and the two cars. The upper half of Avinash's body protruded from under the blasted hulk of the bus's front portion, his guts spilling onto the ground around him. Lying on his back, he looked up at her and the vague, massive presence which hovered around her, and which she knew to be Amruteshvar.

He struggled onto his side, and his guts were sucked back into the bloody mess of flesh and clothing that had been his abdomen, which was now magically knitting itself together again. The bus groaned and shifted slightly as he dragged himself from under it, trailing crushed legs which were also rapidly recomposing themselves as the gore that covered them receded and evaporated. He pulled himself onto his arms and knees, paused to collect his strength, then staggered unsteadily to his feet.

Standing amidst the flames, he turned his gaze up to

Nada and Amruteshvar. His face was mild, brown-eyed, completely human. *"Pāhi tām,"* he said in Sanskrit. *Take care of her.*

Then they were rising, leaving Avinash looking up at them, and beyond him, the huge throng of people who had gathered in the street around the burning bus, and who seemed to see the bus alone. The sky had rapidly grown dark with rainclouds, and Nada felt another nearer darkness spread about them like wings as they flew ever higher above the city, over Vetal Tekadi, over the Institute on the other side, and down towards Usha Road. Then the dream faded and she slipped into oblivion, exhausted.

Nada awoke in her room in *Yadnya,* with the sun of evening bathing the wall. She was wearing the same clothes, and could feel the sweat and dirt of the day on her skin. As she turned onto her side, she felt that she ached everywhere, and that she was still weak, even after—what, maybe seven hours of sleep?

She remembered the day's events as far as the flight, a dreamlike memory that was difficult to distinguish from the dreams she had had since then. As she tried to sort out vision and reality, she felt a growing dread of the likely real-world consequences of what had happened.

She had been at the centre of a spectacular disaster, witnessed by hundreds of people, in which many people had been killed. What awaited her when she got up and went downstairs? Would the police be there? If not, they must certainly be on her trail. Hundreds of people had seen her and Amruteshvar getting into the bus after it had crashed off Malati Road; they had seen them involved in the violence that left the passengers and many bystanders dead. Their role in those events, their opposition to Avinash, may not have been clear.

And clownishly inept as the police were, how difficult could it be for them to find her? She had been a frequent and striking sight in this neighbourhood for a quarter of a century. Even many who had never talked with her must have at least heard about her, know where she worked and lived.

And apart from the loss of so many innocent lives, and the appalling question of her role in it, this event was a disaster for her personally. What would it mean for her position in India? Would she be tried and jailed? Expelled? Secretly blacklisted and barred from the country? These were fates of which she had always lived in fear, and she had been so grateful, after losing Zoran, that that most devastating experience of her life had not been compounded by exile from their hearts' adopted homeland, which would certainly have tipped her into suicidal despair.

Then, her own parents and Zoran's had flown from Croatia to help her deal with the police, devastated and drained as she was, and in the background she had had influential support in India and Europe. The police had not been inclined to cause difficulties. Nothing in her bizarre story had corresponded to anything real. Even the villages, roads, temples, and countryside she had described did not exist, and Zoran's body had been found on the side of the highway with a massive head wound.

It was obvious to the police what had happened: clearly this foreign girl had been driven temporarily mad by the trauma of seeing her boyfriend struck and killed by a passing vehicle, and besides, they had probably both been stoned for weeks. So there had been no further investigation, Nada, her parents, and Zoran's parents had gone back to Croatia with his body, and she had had no difficulty at the Indian embassy in Zagreb or the Mumbai airport when she returned to India a few months later.

She doubted she would be so lucky this time. She slipped her feet over the bedside and sat up slowly and painfully, noticing how dirty her clothes were. At that moment there was a knock on the door, and she braced herself for whatever she would have to face next. But the voice that followed was Kamala's.

"Nada, are you awake? Amruteshvar thinks you've just woken up."

Amruteshvar. Yes. He was alive. She had seen him die, horribly, and then... he had been alive again, and had saved her. This had been real. She clung to this certainty with a solid, exhilarating sense of relief and safety.

"Yes, he's right," Nada replied. "Just a minute."

She shook her head and stood up slowly, then went and opened the door.

"How are you feeling?" said Kamala. "Would you like some tea?"

"That would be beautiful, yes," said Nada. "Is it just Amruteshvar downstairs? Is... everything all right?"

"It's just him, yes," replied Kamala. "He told me what happened—not everything, he said, but enough. You both came in the back door around one, just before there was a tremendous thunderstorm, pre-monsoon. You were asleep on your feet. We brought you straight up and put you to bed in your clothes."

As they moved towards the stairs, Nada paused to look in at the door of the study, and saw what she was looking for: the manuscript sat on the desk wrapped in its apparently unscathed red cloth. She went over and picked it up to look at it more closely. There was no sign of its recent adventures—being thrown into the bus by Avinash, being pressed against his bloody shoulder. She put it back down and touched the rosary, then turned and went downstairs with Kamala.

Amruteshvar was sitting on one of the chairs in the hall, and looked up when she came in alone.

"I guess you're feeling a little bad, but not *too* bad," he said.

"Quite right. You know everything, don't you," replied Nada, smiling slightly, her voice touched with irritation, despite the near-joy she had felt on seeing him again, which a confusion of shame and guilt had caused her to repress. "Do you know what the upshot of today's adventure is going to be? The police station is just fifty feet down the road. It may take them a while to figure it out, but I'm sure they'll find their way here eventually."

"In fact they won't," said Amruteshvar. "The city thinks the bus driver went mad after hitting his head in the crash, then took off on his own. You'll read that in the paper tomorrow. The people who saw us... didn't *see* us. Normally, when it's just a few people, this kind of problem isn't hard to take care of, but I have to admit that with the hundreds who saw us this time, it wasn't so easy. But I managed."

Nada sat down in a chair beside him and poured some

water for herself from the metal flask on the table, drinking three cupfuls one after the other, pouring the water directly into her mouth without touching the metal cup to her lips, in the Indian manner. Then she sat with the cup in her hands, staring blankly. "All those people..." she murmured, shaking her head. Her eyes misted. He smiled at her with quiet, deep compassion.

Putting down the cup, she said, "I'm sure you also know that I've been having dreams. I'm not even sure how much of what just happened was a dream."

Amruteshvar was looking at her intently, then let his gaze drop. "I don't think I have to tell you a lot," he said. "You're figuring things out quickly on your own. Things are... coming back to you."

Nada thought of asking more *(What? What is coming back to me?)*, but then realized that she really didn't have to. It was all simple and obvious, wasn't it? An epic of karma of a kind familiar to her from the ancient books. The three of them had been brought together by some event that took place many lives ago, some action which had remained unfinished and which was keeping them bound together until they worked it out and finished it.

What Nada had seen and felt in dream and vision told her that this was a story of love, jealousy, hate—and that she was the centre of it. The *vetala* that had possessed Avinash was some kind of expression of this conflict, or some outside evil that had taken advantage of the break the conflict had caused, slipping in to join itself to the negative emotion in Avinash, corrupting and confusing the man's very self, pushing aside and starving what had been good in it.

It was something like what had happened to King Nala in the famous story in the *Mahabharata*. Nada remembered that Amruteshvar himself had made the comparison once. She would talk to him about this, tonight.

Kamala returned from the kitchen with tea on a tray. Nada and Amruteshvar took their cups, and Kamala went out, leaving them alone.

Suddenly remembering, Nada said, "Shyamala was supposed to come this afternoon. Did she?"

"Yes," replied Amruteshvar. "I told her you had unexpectedly felt extremely tired and gone to bed, and that she should come tomorrow afternoon instead."

"God, what will she think of me?" sighed Nada. "And what are *we* going to do? What is there for us to do, besides wait for Avinash to make his next attack? I don't even know yet how we can free him. I guess that's going to be one of those things that you said I have to figure out for myself."

Amruteshvar smiled slightly, apparently a little embarrassed.

"I'm afraid so," he said. "But you're very good at that. And you still haven't finished reading the last chapter. It will tell you everything you need to know."

"I *have* read it through rapidly, which is how I know about the defective verse. But there is so much in it that is not clear. I was looking forward to months of hard work. Fortunately, I have you here now," she said a little ironically. "And presumably you *can* tell me *something,*

91

can't you? Otherwise why would you have come at all?"

He smiled again, and looked down, and they sipped their tea in silence.

When they had gone upstairs to the study, Nada opened the manuscript on the desk, divided the palm leaves into two stacks where she thought the last chapter must begin, added leaf by leaf to the larger stack until she had found it. They sat on opposite sides of the desk, facing each other, and paused.

Then Amruteshvar said, "I wrote this book in order to try to understand what had happened to my brother. There was nothing like it in Sanskrit before. I took some information from Sanskrit and other texts on various subjects, but mainly I was compiling and synthesizing what I had learned from the people I was talking to, both Brahmins and non-Brahmins, scholars and non-scholars, people who came close to *bhuts* and *prets*, ghouls and ghosts, in their work as funerary ritualists, magicians, physicians, astrologers. Even common, illiterate people could tell me so much that there was no trace of in books. And I put all this into Sanskrit for the first time."

Yes, she was thinking, *yes*. She knew this—and here it was. Her mind was infused with a paradoxical alloy of exhilaration and deep calm which pressed aside her awareness of everything else—the shock and slaughter of the chase, the impending threat of Avinash's inevitable reappearance.

Amruteshvar was still speaking. "But one of the

most important keys *was* actually a Sanskrit text: the *Nalopakhyana,* the Tale of King Nala in the *Mahabharata.* It taught me exactly how my brother had gotten ill, exactly what the relation of his self to his illness was. As you know, King Nala is possessed by Kali, Confusion. Kali undermined and corrupted Nala's self in the same way that the *vetala* did to my brother. When Nala abandoned his beloved wife Damayanti, his will was partly his own and partly Kali's; the reasons he gave himself for abandoning her were his own, but he was also being driven by the alien incubus that was determined to destroy him. The same thing happened to my brother, but in his case there was another cause beside the generic malice of Manyu, Rage. My brother hated me, because we loved the same woman. And that was the *dosha*—the fault, the sin—that gave the spirit of evil its opportunity to invade him."

He paused, almost as if he expected Nada to raise some question or objection, as in the past. But Nada knew that he couldn't really expect this. There was nothing more that she needed to ask. And she knew he knew that. Otherwise there would have been no point in telling her what he was telling her. Now was the time to listen.

He went on. "When the book was finished, it turned out to have a power different from what I had hoped. It did not help me drive the evil from my brother. It was the sum of everything I had been able to learn about the *vetala,* but knowledge on its own turned out not to be enough. Because I had my own *dosha*—the same as my brother's, in fact, but I guess the spirit entered him and not me because his fault was greater, his love and hate deeper and more conflicted. And that was always what had distinguished us, twins though we were: he was deeper in everything."

Amruteshvar's face showed the expressionless seriousness that it always wore. And yet Nada could almost have believed that it was suffused, almost imperceptibly, with the same serene joy that she was feeling, and that was perhaps visible in her own.

"So I could not be the one to use the knowledge that I myself had assembled," said Amruteshvar. "But that knowledge turned out to have a power that I had not foreseen: in the physical form of this book, it was a *weapon*, dangerous in itself, capable of harming and terrorizing the *vetala,* if not of destroying him. Only in the right hands could the knowledge destroy. And as I eventually realized, there was only one right pair of hands."

He was finished. And Nada knew it.

She said, "So our chapter is *Amrutashamana.* Shall we begin at the beginning?"

Amrutashamana, "Laying the Undead to Rest," was the name of the final chapter, the last of ten which purported to give a comprehensive account of the *vetala*—or, as the text no less frequently called him, turning an ancient term for divinity on its head, the *amṛta,* "the undead."

The ten chapters were:

Amṛtasaṃbhava, "Origin of the Undead";
Amṛtavasana, "Where the Undead Lives";

Amṛtāhāra, "What the Undead Eats";
Amṛtaśakti, "Powers of the Undead";
Amṛtaśarīravṛtti, "The Physical Nature of the
     Undead";
Amṛtasaṃtati, "How the Undead Reproduces";
Amṛtacitta, "The Mind of the Undead";
Amṛtābhijñāna, "Recognizing the Undead";
Amṛtanivāraṇa, "How to Ward Off the Undead";
and *Amṛtaśamana.*

Over more than twenty years, Nada had worked
through nine chapters, reading on her own, with Kshirasagar, and in the beginning also with Zoran, and together she and Kshirasagar had produced an annotated translation of them. They had been working separately on the
Amrutashamana when he died, and the first order of business for Nada and Shyamala was to conflate their existing
work on this chapter; then they would have to translate
and annotate the remainder, a process which would have
taken an unknown number of months, maybe years.

This work would have been more slow and difficult
without Kshirasagar and his consummate mastery of language and history, but with the end so close, and the present necessity so strong, Nada would have been driving
herself harder than they had done before, and Shyamala—who in the work thus far had fully lived up to Bhate
and Nada's favourable impression of her—would surely
have continued to prove a worthy accomplice.

Maybe Kshirasagar had also felt an urgency as his own

end neared: comments he had made to Nada in his last year, in emails and in person, hinted that he knew that any day could be his last. But his anxiety would have been different from the one that drove Nada now. For Kshirasagar, finishing the edition of the *Amrutajijnasa* meant resuscitating a lost ancient account of an evil that had dealt him a lingering death stroke. Perhaps by so doing he could save unknown victims in the future, but he could not save himself, nor could he save his destroyer—and in any case, the *vetala* was to them a creature of pure and simple evil in those days, a monster that had wrecked both their lives.

For Nada, there was now a much more immediate motive for finishing the edition: her own present protection, yes, and the exorcism of the event that had been the defining trauma of her life; but also, no less importantly, the salvation of the monster himself, who had unexpectedly been revealed as the tragic protagonist of the *Amrutajijnasa.*

Avinash had a history with earlier chapters, in which he was a good man, with a brother and a family; in which he was a lover—perhaps, like her, bereaved in love, but in any case a victim of the *vetala* no less than she herself. Avinash, she now realized, was someone to be loved. A man she could herself imagine loving.

Nada and Kshirasagar's practice had been to make their own separate translations during the greater part of the year, while Nada was in Zagreb, and then, while Nada was in Pune from May to September, to reread the text and conflate their translations, then proceed together beyond the point where their finished work ran out.

Now, Nada divided her days between conflating the translations with Shyamala, beginning at eleven in the morning, and translating with Amruteshvar, from four in the afternoon. The *Amrutashamana* contained a hundred and twelve *shlokas,* verses. Nada had translated and annotated fifteen, Kshirasagar twenty-two. So Nada and Amruteshvar had read the original text from the beginning, then begun their translation at verse sixteen.

Reading the text with Amruteshvar was a new and strange experience. With Kshirasagar, Nada had always felt the silent presence of a vast erudition which would reveal itself in unhesitating corrections, comments, and explanations that unostentatiously intimated the vastness of the store from which they emerged.

With Amruteshvar, that presence felt infinitely vaster. He had, after all, written the *Amrutajijnasa,* but it was more than that: he embodied the world in which this book was born, a world which was only very faintly reflected in even the deepest present-day *panditya*—traditional Sanskrit learning—to say nothing of the yet more emaciated erudition of English-based academic scholarship.

Sitting at the desk with the manuscript in front of her, Nada would read the *shloka* aloud and translate it; then Amruteshvar, seated behind her and to her right, with eyes closed, would repeat her translation with corrections; then she would write this version down, with pen in notebook, an old-fashioned practice to which Kshirasagar had stuck even after becoming computer-literate, and to which Nada had also become loyal.

It was at this point that their new method most sharply diverged from the old. Over the years of their collaboration, Nada and Kshirasagar, after finalizing the translation of each verse, had then proceeded to spend a good deal of time, sometimes hours, consulting a small pile of works which they had found to have anything to say about *vetalas,* and incorporating that matter into the note on the verse.

With Amruteshvar, the books sat idle on the shelf, and even when he did cite some of them in the course of his commentary—delivered clearly and unhesitatingly, as if reading finished text from a page, but with eyes closed—they no longer seemed the distinguished authorities they once had, being outnumbered now by a much larger collection which had evidently survived nowhere but in the vast library of Amruteshvar's memory.

And they were superseded not only in number: that little pile of books—the *Mahabharata*, a few other major Sanskrit works, plus a handful of obscure old printed texts and encyclopedias in Sanskrit, Hindi, and Marathi—seemed wretchedly meagre in comparison with the ones that dominated Amruteshvar's commentary, books on astrology, alchemy, black magic, and medicine that had had a great deal to say about *vetalas* and upon which the *Amrutajijnasa* was directly based.

For Nada, the new vista that thus opened up was at once intoxicating and frustrating: her sense of the text's background was infinitely enriched by these citations, yet this enrichment was doomed to remain known to her alone, because citations from a treasure trove of lost and unproduceable texts could have no scholarly credibility. What would the footnote sound like? "I thank Dr. Amruteshvar, an undead scholar from fourteenth-century Mysore, for making these previously unknown works available to me"?

So the list of works cited remained the same as before, and the notes on the verses were not noticeably deepened by this enormous new access of information. But Nada could live with this irony, because scholarship, or at least that kind of scholarship, was no longer the point.

The final chapter, *Amrutashamana,* was about "laying the undead to rest." The term *amṛta* had been defined in the book's first chapter, *Amrutasambhava:*

> *vetālaḥ preta evā 'sti kena cit pratijīvitaḥ*
> *mṛta āsīn mṛto nā 'sti tato 'mṛta iti smṛtaḥ*

> The vampire is a dead man who has been brought back to life by something. He was dead, and is not dead, and therefore is he called *undead.*

The same chapter said that the *vetala* is a spirit who enters and inhabits a living person in the same way that Kali entered King Nala (a simile that the book made much of, and frequently returned to):

> *anyo naro 'mṛto 'nyaś ca yas tv āviśati taṃ naram*
> *tiṣṭhaty anyas tathā 'nyasmin yathā 'tiṣṭhat kalir nale*

99

The man is one, and the undead who enters that man is another: one dwells in the other as Kali dwelt in Nala.

Further on, the possessing spirit was said to be Kali himself, and the *vetala* was evidently the victim, the man possessed:

> *kalir nalam yathā 'viṣṭo vijahāra mano 'lpaśaḥ*
> *vetālasyā 'pi sa tathā haraty ātmānam ātmanaḥ*

As Kali entered Nala and took away his mind bit by bit, so does he take the vampire's self away from his self.

This ambiguity—who is the possessor, who the possessed?—ran throughout the book, but began to be emphasized in the *Amrutashamana,* particularly with respect to the problem of the *vetala's* will and responsibility:

> *anyāviṣṭo hi vetālo na jānāty ātmano manaḥ*
> *ātmano 'pahṛto 'nyena cā 'nyabhūto 'pi cā 'tmanaḥ*

For being possessed, the vampire does not know his own mind: he has been stolen from himself by another, and has become other than himself.

> *na svecchayā naram hanti vetālo me 'ti vismara*
> *vetālo 'pi hi sambaddho mumukṣaty antarātmanā*

The vampire does not of his own volition kill a man:
do not forget this; because the vampire himself is
bound, and longs for release with his inmost soul.

Beyond their literal meaning and literary context,
Amruteshvar never had anything to say about what such
verses might mean, and though their application to Avinash was obvious to Nada, she nevertheless found Amruteshvar's principled silence exasperating sometimes.
But more and more she understood why it had to be this
way: if she had been told outright what she was now piec-
ing together from the text and from her increasingly full
and lifelike dreams—almost a rival reality at this point—
she would never have believed any of it. It had to come
from within her, because it was *there*. And if this much
was there, then everything was there, including the eight
missing syllables that were the key to everyone's freedom.

At night, as she lay naked on the bed amid the shifting
heat and cool of the room, waiting for the precious visions
of dream, aching with a longing of which she was ever
more conscious, she would hear and murmur the words
that mocked her from the far shore that she needed to reach,
where all of them would be happy and at peace, and where
two of them, she now knew, would be reunited in love:

mumukṣuṃ śamayet tu tam

May she lay to rest him who longs for release.

PART TWO

That morning Nada had come to the Institute for the first time in weeks. It was now late July, and the monsoon, crazed and mutilated by climate change, had at last managed to gain a weakened foothold, bringing hard rain to the nights and to part of every day a full month after what had been the normal date of its arrival when Nada had first started to come to India. Though much reduced from the robust classical form in which Nada had come to know it, it was still recognizably the familiar season of clothes never quite dry and umbrellas rarely closed, of shining streets hissing with traffic, of dogs that slept the day away curled and shivering in the refuge of sheltered walls and unused doorways, of a rich greenness that possessed the hills and the Institute's hermitage-like grounds overnight.

Nada's daily life during this period had been even more restricted than in years past, when she and Kshirasagar would work together from dusk to dawn, and Nada, never much of a sleeper, would often find time to move about the city and its vicinity during the afternoons.

Now she slept at night, but the whole day was devoted to work: to the preparation of the edition's text with Shyamala in the mornings, and to translation with Amruteshvar in the afternoons, punctuated by a quiet tea with Kamala several times a day. Her initial work with Shyamala—the combining of Nada and Kshirasagar's work—had finished some time ago, and they had moved on to the typing up of the translation's daily increments and the writing of the introduction.

It was this latter task that had today brought Nada to the Institute, to check a few references in the library which had not been confirmable in Kshirasagar's large personal library at *Yadnya*. It felt slightly surreal to be venturing this far from the house after weeks in which she had gone no further than the general store and the Sahadev restaurant on Usha Road. During this period she had felt a strange and unexpected serenity.

Avinash had not reappeared after the day of the hijacking; there had been no word from the police; and Nada had gratefully allowed herself to be entranced by the rhythm of her daily work over the whispering illusion of silence that the rains always brought to the city.

The dreams, too, played their part in the growth of this mood: the terror and menace that had pervaded them in the beginning had given way to a comforting familiarity as their images, even the dreadful ones, had settled into a predictable series of scenes, which now felt almost like silent, sympathetic witnesses to Nada's quest, contributing to the sense of imminence and promise of those days.

On reaching the Institute at ten-thirty, Nada first stopped in the main building to see if Vimala had arrived yet; finding that she had not, she came back out by the front door so that she could walk round the main building to the library behind, enjoying the springtime luxuriance that the monsoon had awakened in the Institute's grounds. A spray of light rain was in the air, and in the east a patch of clear sky was visible which would soon bring a few moments of sunshine. Everything that had been some shade of brown a month before was now some shade of green.

The traffic on Malati Road was scarcely visible through the thick screen of bushes and low trees. The façade of the guest house was alive with rejuvenated ivy, and the area beyond it that had briefly been leased as a plant nursery a decade before was now a jungle whose untrodden undergrowth had almost completely claimed the broken bottles and burned garbage left in the winter by the groundskeepers' teenage children.

A dog whom Nada knew to be habitually unfriendly observed her from where he lay at the margin of the groundskeepers' colony, and the colony's single rooster and his hens pecked and strutted before its small waist-level shrine to the elephant-headed god Ganapati, more revered in Maharashtra state than anywhere else in the country.

Behind loomed Vetal Tekadi, Vampire Hill, a haunt of monkeys and deer where Nada had used to walk with Zoran in the early days, but which she had rarely visited since then (having been there most recently when Avinash drove the bus off its peak). High grass had sprung up around the lotus pond behind the main building, vying with the thickets of vegetation that thrived year-round beside the tanks of drinking water on the covered walkways. Another dog was sleeping on the library's bottom step when she went in.

No one was in the main hall except a familiar assistant, who lounged half-sleeping on his wooden chair against the wall and smiled at her in recognition. Planning to browse the journals before she searched the card catalogue, she entered the reading room, and had just begun to page through one of them when she heard someone call her name.

"Nada!"

She looked up to see a white man sitting at one of the old wooden tables, the only other person in the room. He was about sixty-five, but his fit, almost heroic physique, his full head of curly white hair, and a strange aura of youthfulness gave the impression of an eternal adolescence, made stronger by the unguarded happiness that now lit up his face.

"I should have expected to see you here at this time of year!" he said, rising to his full height of six-two.

Nada felt her face flood with what must have seemed an almost comical joy. Of course, it was Saul, Saul Levitt, an American Sanskrit professor who was one of her oldest friends, and whose love for Pune, where he had lived and studied for many years, was a special bond with her. She had been so sunk in her struggle with Avinash and the *Amrutajijnasa* that she had completely forgotten what

Bhave had told her on the first day about Saul's impending stay at the Institute. She felt a piercing regret for the loss of the consolation that this knowledge would have afforded her over these difficult weeks, if she had remembered.

She opened her mouth to speak, but no words came. He paused for a moment, then seemed to understand, and came and stood in front of her, smiling.

"I'm in the guest house, of course," he went on. "I got here three days ago from Mumbai. Before that I was up north in Uttarakashi, since June. You know I've built a house there? Don't really have any serious business I need to do in Pune this time, but you know I always stop here on my way south: so many people and places here I always want to touch base with. And I've got two articles to write, and this is always a good place for writing."

Nada continued to stare at him open-mouthed, embarrassed by her absurd silence, but unable to articulate her happiness. She realized that she hadn't had a real conversation in weeks with anyone but Amruteshvar and Shyamala, and after so much time talking about nothing but how to kill vampires in Sanskrit, she was finding it difficult to think of the right words for this situation.

It didn't matter: Saul could talk enough for both of them.

His smile faded. "Hey, I heard about Kshirasagar. It actually wasn't mentioned in the online groups, I didn't hear about it till Vimala Bhave told me when I arrived. You know I knew him too. Back in the seventies he knew everyone, and all us foreigners, but then he got sick, and most of us he never saw again. But I saw him every few years, down at his house—yeah, a couple of times you were there too. But no one was closer to him than you, obviously. Really made me sad when I heard about it. But Vimala was right, it was as much a blessing as anything."

Nada was still smiling, but now tears began to flow, and she let out a soft sound which was both a laugh and a sob, averting her eyes from his.

"Ah Nada," said Saul, and hugged her, and she hugged him back, rapidly becoming aware of how much pain she still carried over this loss. Amruteshvar was not exactly a great consoler, and anyway, after his early confessions about his history with Avinash, the focus with him had always been the text. And Kamala, like Nada, was a silent griever, a habit she had probably cultivated as a result of always having had so little family to depend on.

But at last, Nada found words: "Let's go over to the Hutatma."

"Yeah, great idea," said Saul. "Let's hurry before they replace it with a Costa Coffee or some other such abomination."

He turned back to his table, packed up his laptop, left an already-written note on top of the pile of books he was using, and together they walked out, regarded curiously by the assistant half-sleeping on his chair.

The clear patch of sky Nada had seen to the east was now overhead, and sunlight briefly held the field. The bell would soon be rung for the day's first tea break, and a few people were now to be seen here and there.

"I'm writing a paper on a spirit possession I attended in Andhra Pradesh a few months ago," said Saul, as they started walking towards the Institute's main gate. "I don't know if you've had the chance to read any of my work in recent years?"

"Of course," she said, still finding it a little difficult to get the words out. "I read everything you write."

"Then you'll know that that's the subject I've been working on the most lately, possession," he said. "Always too many pans on the stove!"

He smiled, and she smiled with him.

"My interest in that goes back to the seventies," he said, "to when my wife and I used to roam around the countryside on foot in search of sacrifices. In one village we came to in Andhra Pradesh, there was a possession going on: people possessed by the spirits of the Pandavas and Draupadi, from the *Mahabharata*. It was ritualized, dramatized, you know?—with scenes from the *Mahabharata* acted out."

Shyamala rode through the main gate on her scooter.

"Hey Shyamala!" Saul shouted.

"You know her?" asked Nada, a little surprised, but not very, since Saul got to know everyone eventually.

"Oh yeah, of course. She's quite the up-and-coming young star, isn't she. I know she's working with you on your text—what's it called, the *Vetalajyotsna* or something?"

At this, Nada stopped in her tracks and doubled over, laughing and laughing in a fit of cathartic release. This was such a typical Saul Levitt joke: *jyotsna,* moonlight, was a common name for Sanskrit commentaries because of the idea of illumination, but combined with *vetala,* the name it produced—"Moonlight of the Vampire"—was almost unbearably funny.

"The *Vetalajyotsna!* Oh god, Saul, I love it."

"What, that's not what it's called?" said Saul, smiling, gratified by the effect of his pretended gaffe, so emblematic of his peculiar genius.

Nada was in tears of hilarity by the time Shyamala approached, smiling but mystified.

"Nada and I were just talking about possession, and then I guess she started giving a demonstration," Saul said to Shyamala. "We were on our way to the Hutatma. Can you join us?"

"Sure," Shyamala replied, and they proceeded out the main gate.

When they had sat down and ordered tea, and Nada had recovered herself, she turned to Saul and said, "So you were telling me about this possession you attended in Andhra Pradesh ages ago, and then you attended another one there more recently, which you're writing about?"

"Yeah, but the two aren't connected," he replied. "The later one wasn't related to anything in Sanskrit: the possession was by a local divinity, a goddess, who entered a female medium. It was a medical ritual: the god-

112

dess was a disease who had infected several people in the village. But my perspective on these possessions is always fundamentally sanskritic, because *I'm* fundamentally sanskritic, and there's so much about possession in Sanskrit literature, more than people realize—certainly more than anthropologists realize. You know, I have no formal anthropological training, all my degrees are in Sanskrit. But I've spent more time 'in the field,' in *this* field, than most anthropologists, because,"—he sipped his tea—"the field is where I live."

It was true. Saul had always been the Indiana Jones of academic Sanskrit studies, a discipline he had entered mainly in order to fund his long periods of wandering around India with a knapsack full of Sanskrit books. Nada had largely modelled her career on his.

"But I'm too close to this right now because I'm writing about it," he said. "I need a break. I don't really know much about the book you guys are working on, the... *Amrutajijnasa*, right? Have I finally remembered it right?"

Nada laughed. "You never really forget anything, Saul." She glanced at Shyamala, who was sitting quietly, as if she didn't want to be noticed, evidently fascinated by this old friendship between her admired senior colleague and another extraordinary scholar.

"What a weird use of the word *amṛta*," he said. "It's unique, so far as I know: elsewhere it always means something immortal or divine, particularly the divine nectar, of course. But here, it really is like a direct translation of the English word 'undead.' Do you know where *that* word comes from? Is it in other European languages? Like Croatian?"

Nada nodded. Then she said: "Our work has... taken a new turn lately."

She was longing to open up to Saul about what had been happening. Now that Kshirasagar was gone, Saul was really the only person in the world who could understand. In fact, he would be able to completely understand everything, intellectually and personally. He knew almost everything about her, even the business with Avinash. But so much had happened since Kshirasagar had died, so much had been revealed, and it was all so incredible and terrible.

Saul would believe her, he alone had seen enough to know that everything that was happening to her was possible and real. And by now Shyamala had become a friend, and knew or suspected enough that Nada felt she could tell her as much as she could tell Saul. But how to begin?

"We're now working with the scholar who is the ultimate authority on the *Amrutajijnasa* and *vetalashastra*. He contacted me on his own. He and I are finishing the translation. He's given us profound insight into the text, and especially into its historical background. There's a tragic story behind it."

"You'll have to tell me about this 'ultimate authority,'" said Saul. "I've probably met him. But who's this text attributed to?"

"A certain Amruteshvar," said Nada, "who lived in a village near modern Mysore in the fourteenth century.

He had a twin brother. Avinash."

At this, a flicker of concern passed across Saul's face.

"Both were brilliant scholars," Nada continued. "Superstars of their time, really: young, brilliant, beautiful. Not really rivals, but almost, they *could* have been. Avinash was engaged to be married to a girl named Lata. And Amruteshvar fell in love with her. He didn't do or even say anything, but he fell in love with her, and it became obvious to both Avinash and Lata. It corrupted the brothers' relationship, and Avinash's mind."

She felt her words tumbling forth, released. Saul and Shyamala were staring.

"It was just like the way Kali entered King Nala, you know, in the *Mahabharata?* Just like that. Avinash began to change. He'd always been this very gentle and good person, but now he started attacking his brother, first verbally, then even physically. Everything that had been good and beautiful about him became corrupted and poisoned. He became suspicious of Amruteshvar and Lata. And she killed herself, she hanged herself." Nada was crying. "And then Avinash killed himself too."

There was a long pause. Saul and Shyamala sat speechless. Then Saul asked, "How do you know all this? Is the story told in the text?"

"No," said Nada. "Amruteshvar told me the basics, but then I... found out the rest on my own, and... I *know.*"

"Amruteshvar...?" said Saul. "The *author of the text?* How...?"

Nada looked him in the eye, and with that he understood.

"I know this story," Saul said.

"How...?" said Nada, almost whispering.

"I've read it," he said, "and I've also *seen* it. Once. In a village in south Karnataka. A possession. There's a tradition down there, very small and local. They tell a story, this very story that you've just told me: the souls of these three enter people, and they re-enact it. I found out about it through friends in Mysore. I was allowed to witness it, and was working on an article about it, but I put it aside for the time. It was going to be a lot of work, it would have to be a series of articles, because there were also *texts,* like I was saying: tellings of the story in Kannada, Tamil, and Malayalam, but also one in Sanskrit, which they actually have in the Institute library right here."

"I... I've never heard of this before," Nada murmured.

"I'm not surprised," he said. "This is a very small local tradition; no one, Indian or non-Indian, has ever written about it. It was really a scoop for me, but I was going to have to keep coming back to it for years. And you know, I'm always doing too many things at once."

"What's in the library here?" asked Shyamala. "It's a printed book?"

"Yeah," said Saul, "old, like from the thirties. What's it called... aha, just *Avinashalatacharita,* The Story of Avinasha and Lata. It's short, a few hundred verses, no chapter divisions, easy Sanskrit. That edition has a short preface in Sanskrit, but I don't remember it, don't remember if it says when the poem was written. Come on, let's go find it for you! We can ask Bhave to let us take it to the manuscript department and compare it with what your book says—oh, but you say the story isn't told there."

"Why... would we take it to the manuscript department?" asked Nada. "The *Amrutajijnasa* is at home, at *Yadnya*."

Saul looked incredulous. "But there's another copy of the *Amrutajijnasa* in the manuscript department! You mean you didn't *know*?"

9

AN ANCIENT TALE

"Hello...?" said Nada tentatively, knocking lightly on the swinging wooden divider that served as a door to the general secretary's office. "Dr. Bhave?"

"Yes, hello," came Vimala Bhave's voice from the other side. "Is that you, Nada? Please come in."

Nada pushed on the divider, which swung inward with a creak of expanding metal springs.

Bhave looked up from where she was sitting at her desk. "Ah, and it's not only Nada, but also Shyamala and Saul Levitt!" she said, turning in her seat, smiling with pleasure. "Nada, I haven't seen you in weeks! I was going to write you an email and let you know that Saul had arrived, so I'm happy to see that you've found each other."

Nada smiled. "Yes, I've been out of touch, totally absorbed in the work Shyamala and I are doing. And it's actually in connection with that work that we've come here at this particular moment."

She glanced at Saul and Shyamala. "Saul has just told

118

us about a book in the library that Shyamala and I didn't know about, and that has extremely important implications for our work on the *Amrutajijnasa*. Could you...?" She let her voice trail off.

"You want me to take it out for you? Of course!" said Bhave, tapping the desk with both hands. "We'll go over there now." As she rose, she said, "I'm not at all surprised that Saul was able to help you in this way. Despite all the poor organization and record-keeping, I think he must know our collections better than anyone here." Saul smiled in embarrassment as Nada and Shyamala shot him an admiring glance.

They walked through the north wing to the back door, and crossed to the library in the light rain. Nada gave Bhave the slip of paper on which she had written the book's title and call number, and with only a few civil but commanding words to the head and assistant librarians, Bhave accomplished what would otherwise have been all but impossible: the issuing of a book to a member of the Institute who did not belong to the highest rank of its hierarchy. The three of them thanked Bhave profusely, and she breezed out of the library with her usual regal step.

At Nada's suggestion, they had not mentioned the second copy of the *Amrutajijnasa* to Bhave. Nada was disoriented by the twin revelation of the previously unknown book and the previously unimaginable second manuscript, but not so much that she did not think of the danger: Avinash could be anywhere, and they could not know how long it would take to search for the manuscript in the manuscriptorium's oblivion-shrouded obscurity, how successful the search would be, and whether they would be allowed to take it with them even if they found it.

Of course, Avinash could also be in their own minds—he was certainly in some part of Nada's, at least—but he was sure to learn everything when they actually began searching, whereas there was at least some possibility that his knowledge would remain incomplete for as long as they didn't make a move.

Nada needed time to digest this new development. Because this was definitely the final act, the final element of the plot. Whatever else they might discover in the new manuscript, they would certainly find one thing at least: the missing third quarter of the mutilated verse, the eight syllables that were the key to Avinash and Nada's freedom. The *vetala* was cornered, and he would fight like the desperate creature he was.

"I think I need to be alone with this book," said Nada to Saul and Shyamala, holding the thin, brittle volume. "And... I don't know how long I'm going to take."

They were looking at her with solemn concern—and resignation.

"I'm here in the library till closing time," said Saul. "Come talk to me before you go home."

"I'll be here too for a while," said Shyamala. "And in any case, we'll be seeing each other tomorrow morning at the usual time."

Nada nodded, smiling weakly, then turned and went out the door.

Nada took the thin volume and sat on the steps of the library's second, unused entrance. The rain had stopped. Every few moments, the scene was bathed in sunlight, and the paths were beginning to dry.

The book was just as Saul had remembered it: the *Avinashalatacharita*, 1934, Mysore, Sanskrit introduction. The poem itself consisted of 312 verses of straightforward Sanskrit, written, according to the introduction, by one Vasuki who lived in Mysore in the eighteenth century. In all of her vast reading, Nada had never once encountered a mention of this book: such were the miraculous discoveries that could occur in the still largely unmapped terrain of India's libraries and archives.

Reading the poem, Nada had the feeling of returning to her own forgotten words: to some lost masterpiece of youth which now seemed too flatteringly brilliant to be hers, or a rediscovered journal that decades later shockingly confirmed and validated a lifetime of uncomprehending agony by restoring the long-suspected facts to light:

There was a Brahmin, Avinasha by name, young, handsome, skilled in speech, one who had attained the far shore of the Veda, who delighted in the wellbeing of all creatures. He had a brother, his twin, seemingly equal to him in everything, known as Amruteshvara. Dear to each other as their own lifebreath, in recitation of the Veda, in teaching of the texts, in performance of sacrifice and rituals, they were always together. In debate, no one could defeat them. In mastery of the texts, they had no equal except each other. They seemed to people to be a single man divided into two. No one could see any difference between them. But there was a difference: Avinasha was more passionate and kindhearted, stronger in anger and desire. But between them there was no occasion for dispute, and they carried out their work in complete unity.

When they reached the age of marriage, their father urged them to choose from among the girls of the Brahmin village. There was a girl, Lata by name, the daughter of a scholar who had attained the far shore of the Veda. Dark, tall, intelligent, pure in mind, she came to love Avinasha as she heard him expound the histories and ancient tales to the women day by day. Avinasha, completely absorbed in study, did not notice that Lata had fallen in love with him. But others noticed, and Amruteshvara noticed, and he told him, and from that day Avinasha began to observe Lata when she came with the other women every evening to hear him expound the histories and ancient tales.

One evening, Avinasha began to tell the story of the Ramayana: how Rama won Sita by breaking Shiva's bow, how he married her and took her to Ayodhya, how she followed him to the forest when he was exiled, how he searched for her when she had been abducted by Ravana the demon king, how he invaded the island of Lanka with the army of monkeys and bears and killed Ravana in battle, how he returned with her in joy to Ayodhya and ruled for many thousands of years. In this *way, telling and listening to the story of Rama and Sita's love, Avinasha and Lata fell in love with each other without even having spoken to each other, and their love grew day by day, observed by everyone. They seemed to everyone to be as like to each other in every way as Avinasha and Amruteshvara were, like one person divided into male and female. At last, Avinasha and Lata's fathers, seeing their love, agreed to their marriage, and the date of the wedding was set on an auspicious day.*

Everyone was happy for the imminent marriage of Avinasha and Lata, and Amruteshvara too was happy, because he loved his twin brother as he loved his own lifebreath. But while observing Lata amongst the women who came to listen to Avinasha, while observing her beauty and intelligence, and her passion for his brother, and the growth of their love, Amruteshvara too fell in love with her, and began to burn with impossible desire. As the day of the marriage drew near, Avinasha began to notice that his brother had changed. While studying together, while performing sacrifices and rituals together, even while eating together, Avinasha noticed that something was tormenting and confusing his brother's mind. He knew his brother's mind as he knew his own, and so it was not long before he realized that Amruteshvara had also fallen in love with Lata.

Then, seeing the opening offered by his suspicion, Manyu, Rage, entered Avinasha, and he began to hate his brother. By many signs and hints, Amruteshvara could see that Avinasha's mind had changed towards him, and this saddened and tormented him, because although he too loved Lata, he was not seeking her for himself: he loved his brother more than he loved his own lifebreath, and so he was happy for their love. Burned by remorse, one day Amruteshvara confronted his brother when he happened to meet him in the forest.

"Why do you hate me?" he asked him. "I am not your enemy. I am your brother. I do not wish harm to either you or her."

But Avinasha was enraged, and would not listen, and walked on without replying.

Manyu had entered Avinasha, and began to nurture the defect created by his doubt. Day by day, Manyu swallowed more of Avinasha's mind as Rahu the demon of eclipse slowly swallows the sun. While reading, while writing, while reciting, while expounding, even while eating, walking, and sleeping, Avinasha was burning with suspicion and hate. Lata saw how Avinasha was being swallowed by Manyu. She longed for the day of marriage to arrive, because then, she thought, Manyu would weaken and leave him. Avinasha loved her as much as ever, but now even his love was corrupted by Manyu, because he never ceased to fear that Amruteshvara was about to take her from him. Seeing this, Lata began to despair. Burned by remorse, she felt that it was she who had corrupted Avinasha's love both for her and for his brother. As Avinasha went more and more into the power of Manyu, so Lata went more and more into the power of despair.

Seeing that his brother's torment was only increasing, Amruteshvara wondered what he could do to save him. He began to believe that some evil spirit must have entered Avinasha, and he resolved to gain control over this spirit *through understanding. He began to read books about spirits, demons, and vampires, and to talk to people who knew about them, people both literate and illiterate, noble and common, who knew the science of dealing with spirits. He began to collect what he learned from books and people into his own book, hoping that when he had collected all he could, this book would become the weapon with which to drive the spirit out of Avinasha. He no longer met Avinasha. Each pursued his own work alone, and others were afraid to even mention them to each other.*

Lata fell deeper and deeper into the power of despair. It was as if she too, like Avinasha, had gone into the power of some evil spirit, but in fact it was only the power of her love for Avinasha that was destroying her. The day of the marriage neared, but Avinasha only hated and suspected his brother more and more. Finally, Lata ceased to believe that Manyu would ever release Avinasha, and she lost hope altogether. Believing herself to be the cause of Avinasha's madness and the division between the brothers, completely overcome by despair, she hanged herself.

When Avinasha found her, the horror and remorse that arose in his inmost soul were so powerful that they overwhelmed Manyu, and drove him back to the margin of his mind. For a moment, Avinasha was again fully in possession of himself. With a mind suddenly cleared, he saw how Manyu had possessed and corrupted him, and deluded him into hating his brother and destroying his happiness with Lata. Like a tree struck by Indra's thunderbolt, he fell down on the ground, crying out and weeping. Realizing that Manyu had destroyed him, he resolved to destroy himself and Manyu. Saying tvām anugacchāmi, "I follow you," he hanged himself right next to Lata, and their souls went together to the next world. But Manyu also followed Avinasha: even after death, Manyu clung to his soul, following him from birth to birth as Avinasha, Lata, and Amruteshvara were born together again and again.

Amruteshvara lived on for many years after the deaths of Avinasha and Lata. He never married, but lived alone, performing the work of a Brahmin, and continuing to write his book. As the years passed, he understood more and more deeply what had happened to his brother. But he came to realize that even if he had known then what he knew now, he would not have been able to save Avinasha and free him from Manyu. Only Lata could have done that, if she had understood.

So he finished his book, to be a weapon of knowledge for the future. He also studied other lore, and made himself a master of magic and demonology. Over time, he became as powerful as any vampire, and learned to do everything that a vampire or demon could do. He facilitated many exorcisms, helping the loved ones of the vampires' victims to drive the vampires out. But he could not drive them out himself. At last, being very old, he lay down to die, saying tvām anugacchāmi, I follow you.

Nada lowered her head, and wept.

10

THE MISSING WORDS

Pounding fistfalls on the house's front door dragged Nada out of dreamless sleep as if out of deep water. She raised her head from the desk, where she had sat reading the *Avinashalatacharita* through the evening until she could read no more.

She looked around, saw darkness through the window, and the alarm clock on the bookshelf that told her it was twenty past midnight. The pounding continued, massive and irregular as thunder, and then she heard the voice, *"Nada! Nada!"*

It was Saul.

She started from the chair, stumbled into the passageway and down the stairs in the weak light from the study, unlocked the door as the assault on it continued outside.

"Nada!"

Opening the door, she saw Saul standing with both fists raised, hesitating like a sleepwalker surprised, an expression of confusion and frantic terror on his face.

127

His skin and clothes were patched with dirt, and round his neck was tied a sari, which hung at his back and loosely wound round his calves and feet.

"Saul! What's happened to you?" she gasped, laying her hands on his shoulders, caressing his face, gently leading him over the threshold and into the hall, where Kamala was sitting up on her pallet, frightened.

Nada seated him on the sofa, then sat in a chair opposite and looked at him. He was beginning to come back from whatever nightmare had swallowed him. The fear was ebbing from his face as he slowly realized, it seemed, that he had succeeded in escaping into the care of friends.

"Saul, what happened?" she said. "You look like someone tried to kill you."

He replied with a direct look that told her that this was exactly right. And with that, she understood everything.

Nada turned to Kamala with the most reassuring look she could muster, and said to her in Marathi, "Kamala, this is Professor Saul Levitt. Maybe you'll remember him: he's been in this house before over the years, visiting Dr. Kshirasagar. I met him earlier today at the Institute. He's a close friend, a good person. I don't know what's happened to him now, but I'm sure it must have something to do with Avinash."

Hearing this, Kamala became visibly calmer. "Yes, I... I think I may remember him," she said, looking at Saul.

"Saul, if nothing else, you need some tea," said Nada. "And so do I. What about you, Kamala?"

Kamala shook her head. *"Nako,"* she said. *No.*

Nada got up and went to the kitchen, made tea for Saul and herself, came back with it and sat down opposite him again.

"God, Nada, I can't explain what I've just experienced," Saul began, lifting the tea to his mouth with both trembling hands. "No, I can *explain*. I could even write a paper about it, because I know intellectually what it was. I'd just never *experienced* it before, even though I've had enough opportunities, if any spirit had wanted to take me. I guess I'll *have* to write a paper about it now. It'll be the scoop of my career."

He laughed ironically, sipping his tea.

"Avinash possessed you," Nada said, asking but not asking.

"Oh, is that who it was?" said Saul. "I guess it musta been, who else. Nice guy, pleased to meet him after hearing so much about him."

Another laugh. He gave Kamala a somewhat embarrassed and apologetic look, and her expression of fear faded into an uncertain but sympathetic smile. Then he looked straight into Nada's face, something of the terror of minutes past returning to his own.

"I tried to kill myself," he said. "It was me: all the motivation, all the thinking and memory leading up to it, was mine. But the will was not all my own, there was another will in me, hijacking my mind, my whole *self,* completely occupying and moving it in a way so like myself that I didn't realize what had happened until it released me.

"And I think I know why it released me."

His face and voice became earnest.

"It saw our whole history, Nada, how long we've known and... loved each other, how deep our friendship is. It spared me because I'm precious to you. It spared me because it loves you."

His eyes brimmed with tears, which spilled as he looked down and away from Nada's.

She sat speechless for a while. Neither she nor Saul noticed as Kamala silently left the room.

Then Nada said, softly, "Tell me. Tell me what happened."

"So it was after you left," he began. "Right after we parted from you, Shyamala went home, and I went back into the library. By closing time, 5:30, I was the only one still there. I went out. It was raining again, lightly. There was no one around, besides a groundskeeper who was locking doors at the back of the main building."

He sat a forward on the sofa with hands joined between his knees. He was calmer now, and for the most part stared at the floor in front of him as he spoke, but he was clearly intensely aware of Nada's presence, and from time to time looked up at her with eyes filled with gratitude and faith.

"So I crossed the street to the Hutatma and ordered *idli sambar*. I was planning to be awake for some hours yet, reading and maybe writing again in my room. I'm the only person staying there right now, as so often over the last forty years. In the early days, the place tended to be quite full, but the numbers have fallen off over the years.

"So I finished the *idli,* and ordered tea, and sat half-watching the goings-on around me, the other diners, the staff, the street. I started thinking about how long I've known this place, how the Hutatma has been part of my daily routine during so many critical moments in my life—it's even witnessed a few of them. While I was earning my master's in Sanskrit at the university, for long periods I ate at the Hutatma every evening. And before we were married, Nicole—you know, my first wife?—Nicole and I went there many times with my parents when they were visiting—they used to stay in a huge flat in a side street a five minute walk away.

"On the day Nicole and I were to be married by a local priest in a small Hindu ceremony, on that morning, I sat with her at a table in the upstairs section. And at the last minute—I was so confused and frightened" (he laughed softly)—"I told her that I just couldn't do it, and that I would prefer that we should just be friends. And she wept, and my heart broke for her, and so we went and kept our appointment with the priest after all.

"Another time, sitting at the table right next to the one where I was sitting last night, I opened the letter from my mother telling me that my father had died. My father Professor Levitt. Before he got to see me become Professor Levitt myself."

He shook his head.

"At a table on the other side of the room, Nicole and I had had *idli* and tea one morning before setting out on one of our 'pilgrimages'—that's what we used to call them—one of our pilgrimages around rural Maharashtra and Karnataka, hunting for sacrifices and sleeping by the roadside.

"Upstairs, another time, later, Nicole and I had a spectacular fight, to the embarrassment and amusement of patrons and staff." (Another soft laugh.) "She took the first available flight back to New York two days later—the beginning of the end.

"So I found myself brooding on all this, on what an important place the Hutatma had been in my life. And I felt sad that I would outlive it, it and the Pune it represented to me. I thought of the new house in Uttarakashi in the Himalayas, where I'm planning to retire within a few years, and where I'm planning to die. You know, I've always been more of a southern man. My Marathi and Kannada were once much better than my Hindi. But in this final *ashrama,* this final stage of life, I need the Himalayas."

He smiled, a little sadly.

"So I paid, and went out. It was dark by now. The rain had thinned to a light mist again, it was a beautiful evening, so I decided to stroll a bit on the Institute's grounds before going back to my room.

"The old watchman was sitting on his wooden chair in front of the main building. I know him, he's been around for a few years. I nodded and smiled at him—but not at the upscale young couple with their huge and aggressive golden retriever. You must have seen them before?

Assholes. They bring this dog to the Institute every evening to shit there instead of in the walled yard of their palatial house across the street, and of course no one ever tells them to fuck off."

They both smiled, but Nada remained silent, and he went on.

"The children of the groundskeepers were playing in the treed area between the main building and the library. The teenagers were milling about. Dogs were lounging and wandering around, or standing among the children, watching them play.

"So I reached the guest house, and sat for a while on the damp stone steps in front of my room. And you know, Nada... I've got a tendency to depression, serious depression. I know I've told you before, over the years. It's always there, in the back of my consciousness. I've kept ahead of it for some time now, but under the influence of the events of the day, and these sights and sounds, it started to gain strength, this native melancholy, it started to rise and take possession of my mind. What it does is... the way it gets hold of you... I was starting to think of the totality of my life in a kind of mercilessly detached way. This is how it happens. I knew I was in danger. I tried to turn away from the darkest stuff, the two divorces, tried to think of how fortunate I am to have found Lily—better late than never—someone with whom I can peacefully walk the final stage of the pilgrimage, now that the destabilizing passions of earlier life have burned down to a manageable glow. You know, Nada, I've... never found it easy to find kindred spirits. With her, I feel safe and sure for what's really the first time in my life."

Yes, Nada thought, feeling her eyes mist: depression, the one fatal flaw of this brilliant and good man she had loved and admired for so long. She almost shuddered at the ruthless genius of the evil they were facing.

"But now," he said, "now I was feeling in my guts this cold, nauseating germ of doubt about the worth and dignity of it all—everything, even the best things. This was a very old and familiar experience for me, so I understood what was happening, I knew that there was really nothing to think about here, that this shift was not due to any new information or genuine insight, but to a darkening of the lens. I knew that what I needed was *light,* the light of someone else's company. So I though I might call Lily later, but back in New York it would be too early right now."

Nada smiled, but she felt that if she spoke she would burst into sobs of anguish. "Oh Saul, why didn't you come to find me?" she wanted to ask, but she already knew the answer: he had been too concerned about *her* suffering to allow himself to burden her with his own. So she sat silently and listened.

"I got up. Unlocked my room. Closed the door behind me. Turned on the light, put down my knapsack on the chair, and stood staring vacantly at the scene: the ancient heavy wooden desk, chair, bookshelf, and bed with its mosquito net, the bare stone walls and floor, the door to the washroom, the locked door to the empty main hall. The dust.

"As you know, most Western scholars take one look at these rooms and immediately flee to a hotel. But I've always loved the guest house, this had always been a scene of comfort and safety for me. You know, Nicole and I stayed in a room on the other side, when we were both in India for the first time. We made love there for the first time, with each other or anyone. Those days were just full of love: our love for each other, for India, for its languages and literature... We were discovering it all together, we struggled together for the first time through books that I would return to again and again throughout my life, in Pune and in so many places in India and around the world.

"And... here I was again. I thought, isn't it a profound and beautiful thing, to come back again later and later in life to this place where my journey started? I had always felt that way."

She could relate. And she knew he knew it.

"Yet now, inexplicably, even this scene was clouded with darkness. The darkness had always invested other scenes and memories, and had always lifted when I came back here—and I've actually sometimes come back precisely in order to outrun it when I've felt it rising in me again. But now, for the first time, the sight of all this made me feel... pathetic.

"Pathetic! To be sixty-five years old and to find myself back here again, in this decaying third-world dump" (he winced, ashamed) "—that's how it felt, at that moment—alone, because... what other serious academic would stay

135

here instead of in a hotel or rented flat? To find myself back here, the scene of my first adolescent loves, precisely because... I was still an adolescent, and had never really moved forward or grown up, and everyone else had. I thought, yes, what bullshit is this about 'authenticity' and 'living in the field'? In fact, it was nothing but the typical self-serving auto-mythologization of failure. And I now realized that everyone knew it, and had always known it, everyone except me. I felt like the mist of delusion was rapidly clearing. I saw it all: the indulgent smiles, the shakings of the head, the knowing looks shared between colleagues who I thought were my friends: *Well, that's Saul for you.*"

Again he shook his head. His mouth tightened into a frown.

"I stood there, and... and I felt myself physically falling into the abyss, deeper than ever before. I stared at this room. And it was clearer and clearer to me that it represented my whole worthless life in miniature. I stood there for what felt like a vast period of time. And then my gaze dropped to the bare stone floor, and my despair hardened into conviction. I knew what I had to do. This place, whose true wretchedness was now plain to me, had been the theatre of my story until now. It was also the right place for my story to end."

Nada shook her head.

"The minutes drew out to an eonic length. I kept staring at the floor. After god knows how long, with what felt like... geological slowness, I raised my head and looked at the ceiling fan. My decision had become a force and will of its own. I saw myself... moving slowly and resolutely forward on an unknown course that I nevertheless trusted to be the only true and right one. It was like... an abyss of conscious solipsistic hell gaped on one side of me, and on the other, a truth infinitely superior to my own helpless selfhood offered the perfection of annihilation and oblivion.

"I... my hands... put the chair under the fan. The sari I had bought for Lily... my hands knotted one end of it round my neck, and began to bind the other end round the base of the fan. I knew I wouldn't even pause before kicking the chair away, because... there was nothing to think about. I had had my whole life to think, and the irrefutable conclusion of that life's failed logic had now been revealed to me in the very place where I had struggled for so long to find it."

He smiled ironically. Nada didn't smile.

"Indian philosophy hadn't let me down. I had attained enlightenment. It was time for *moksha,* final release."

A bitter laugh.

"And then... I fell. I dropped hard into the chair. Knocked it sideways and spilled onto the floor with it. Hit my head on the bottom of the bookshelf. I... found myself lying on my back, with my legs bent and turned to the side, and the chair leaning on top of them. The sari had settled over half my face, it was covering my left eye. I looked up at the fan, which was crazily swaying back and forth. I remembered where I was and what I had been doing. But I somehow felt as if I had just now woken up.

The line of thinking of the past minutes or hours now felt like something not quite my own, like a phantom will that had been leading me on towards an end that was at once deeply and originally mine, yet at the same time, paradoxically, alien and new.

"And I could feel... that I was no longer alone. There was another consciousness in the room, invisible and vague, yet tremendously and dreadfully present. And I could feel that it was... confused, consumed by a struggle between pity and hate. While I lay there, waiting for the outcome."

Nada was staring at him, fully present with him, both now and at the moment he was describing.

"I became aware that images from my ancient past with you had been stirred, which I had had no need to consciously revisit in many years: our first meeting here at the Institute; our day-long conversations while walking around the university campus and the countryside near Pune; the hours we've spent together after conferences, sometimes with Victoria—my second wife, you remember her—in European, North American, Indian cities; the times you've visited me at my home in New York; my one visit to yours in Zagreb.

"And seeing all these scenes brought together for the first time, I was struck with a sense of tenderness at the deep intimacy they revealed, and... and I realized that it was to this tenderness that I owed my life: this was what the other presence, whatever it was, was feeling, along with an incomprehensible hatred of me, and rage at having been thwarted by its own pity. And this struggle was still going on, invisible but overwhelmingly present, above and all around me in the room, while I lay waiting—for mercy, fury, madness, death..."

His voice was trembling slightly. He appeared to be struggling to master a rising agitation. And Nada experienced it as her own.

"I was seized by panic. I... scrambled to my feet. I threw myself against the door, burst out of the room, stumbled down the stairs, with the sari... trailing from my neck. I ran down the drive, out the second gate, across Malati Road, down Tilak Institute Road—the streets were empty—down I know not what side streets and lanes, with the sari trailing from my neck, getting tangled around my legs, tripping me..."

He shook his head.

"I just *ran, ran, ran,* tumbling on the ground again and again, getting up again... until I was standing in front of the door of *Yadnya...* pounding on it with both fists..."

His voice was a whisper.

"... screaming your name..."

He was staring at her with shining eyes, his face radiant with terror.

She sat next to him on the sofa for a long time, holding his hand until he became calm again. Kamala entered and quietly sat down.

Then Nada said to Saul, "This happened because he knew that you told us about the second manuscript, which we didn't know about before. I knew he would know that you had told us, because he's around us and he's in our minds, but I didn't know when or how much he would know. And I still don't know what he'll be able to do about it now. He can't touch these manuscripts himself, either in his own body or even in a possessed one, at least not without intolerable pain."

She glanced at Kamala, whose face had darkened with remembrance—and perhaps, too, she thought uncomfortably, with some other kind of distress.

"And he hasn't been able to use possession to get at the first manuscript," Nada went on, "because he can't possess Amruteshvar, or even me, maybe because it would be too painful for him, and no one else gets near it, and anyway, by now he's not as afraid of it, because at some point over the centuries, someone—used by him, obviously—managed to delete that quarter-verse that was the key to the whole book's efficacy."

"And this second copy must have that verse intact," said Saul.

"Right," said Nada, "and so he has to destroy it at all costs. He'll do anything, attempt anything, attempt to possess anyone, at this point, maybe even me and Amruteshvar. We've got to get into the manuscript department—immediately, *tonight.*"

By now Saul had completely recovered, and a growing resolution showed in his face. "But how are we going to get into the Institute now?" he asked.

"I have a key," Nada said. "Bhave gave it to me when

the first manuscript was still there, so that I would feel safer. The guard will be asleep, and even if he sees us we'll probably be able to reassure him. We'll need Amruteshvar—I'm sure he's about to appear out of nowhere at any moment anyway. *Yoo-hoo, Amruteshvar! You can come out now!* And I feel like we should at least tell Shyamala—I feel like it and I don't feel like it, because this will be mortally dangerous, but she would never forgive me if I didn't give her the choice, and there's justice in that."

"Is there anything we should bring?" asked Saul, "Like, garlic, holy water, a figurine of Ganapati? I guess a crucifix wouldn't be very effective."

"Very funny," said Nada, smiling. "Actually, I need you to come with me mainly for comic relief."

They both laughed.

Nada glanced at Kamala, expecting that at least a little of their sudden levity would have communicated itself to her. But Kamala looked even more distressed than she had a moment ago. Something new seemed to be agitating her, something other than the danger that Nada and the others were about to face.

"Kamala," said Nada in Marathi, concerned, comforting. "Don't be afraid. It's true that this will be dangerous, but we will survive, and win. Amruteshvar is very powerful, and now, with this new weapon, this second manuscript, we can't possibly fail. We will certainly destroy the *vetala*. Within hours it will be all over, all these years of fear and suffering."

Kamala shook her head and looked down, and Nada

was shocked to see tears. Kamala had always been so quiet and reserved: although Nada had always felt the depth of her love for her husband and Nada, she had never seen her openly display such strong emotion, and this sight was almost as frightening and ominous to her as Saul's terrible appearance minutes before.

"Nada," Kamala said softly, hoarsely. "This... this second manuscript... Dr. Kshirasagar... he knew about it."

Nada stared at her open-mouthed.

Kamala went on, struggling: "He didn't even tell *me...* but... I came to know. And he told me never to tell. Because..."

She raised her eyes to look straight into Nada's.

"Nada... The danger... It's... very, very great."

Kamala stepped forward and embraced her tremblingly, with a desperate strength. Nada enfolded the much shorter woman in her arms, and stared ahead, filled with a tumult of love and pity, dry-eyed with dread.

Nada phoned Shyamala. Weeks of Sanskrit vampirology and Nada's weird behaviour had no doubt sufficiently prepared the young woman for such a bizarre midnight proposal, and she said she would arrive at *Yadnya* by scooter within the half-hour.

Waiting for her, Nada and Saul sat in silence with Kamala—red-eyed but again outwardly calm—as Saul rapidly read through the *Avinashalatacharita,* softly murmuring the verses to himself.

When Shyamala arrived, the three of them set out

on foot through the deserted streets. At one point, Nada glanced at them, hoping to assess their state of mind, and felt reassured to see that both of them, even Saul, appeared to share her mood of calm determination. From Malati Road they entered the Institute's grounds by a hidden path which would unavoidably bring them within sight of the guard's post in front of the main building.

And there he was, sitting awake, alarmingly, on his wooden chair, looking towards the empty street not far to their left, but evidently not seeing them, even though Nada had immediately stopped short in the most suspiciously guilty-looking way.

"After clouding the minds of hundreds of witnesses to a demonic bus hijacking, this is nothing," said Amruteshvar as he stepped out of the leafy darkness on their right. Nada turned and looked at him with complete unsurprise, and all four laughed softly at the absurd predictability of it.

They proceeded round the back of the main building to the door of the south wing, where Nada took out the key, opened the padlock, gently worked back the bolt and opened the door, and softly closed and bolted it behind them when they had all crept inside.

A weak pale glow from a few scattered tube lights outside shone through the windows and revealed the large room and its contents in basic outline.

"Saul, you said you knew where it would probably be?" Nada whispered, thinking of the guard in front and the groundskeepers' colony not far behind the south wing.

"It will be with the C manuscripts, if it's in the same form as the copy you have. I've never seen it, only a reference to it in some long-forgotten catalogue when I was looking for something else. The C's are over here, in this cabinet."

"It won't be there," said Shayamala in a voice that struck Nada as weirdly hard and cold. "I've seen it before. It's smaller, it's with the D's, over here." She turned on a flashlight and began to move in that direction.

"You've *seen it before*?" said Nada, in a whisper sharpened by incredulity. "Shyamala, why the hell didn't you ever tell me?"

"It's here," repeated Shyamala as if Nada had said nothing, standing in front of one of the heavy wooden cabinets and directing the flashlight's beam through the glass onto a red cloth-bound bundle well above her head.

Saul walked over, opened the cabinet door, reached up and worked the manuscript out from under the several that were piled on top of it.

Except for Amruteshvar, who remained standing in darkness, the three went over to one of the small wooden tables, where Saul untied the cloth ribbon and unwrapped the palm-leaf book.

"*Amrutajanmakatha*," said Saul, reading the title aloud and proceeding to open it at random pages.

"*Amrutajanmakatha*? What?" said Nada, perplexed.

" 'The Story of the Origin of the Divine Nectar,' " Saul said. "This is a poem about the arising of the *amṛta* from the churning of the Ocean of Milk. The title is vaguely similar to *Amrutajijnasa*, but this book has nothing to do with *vetalas*."

He turned and looked at the others blankly.

"I guess this is what you must have seen in the catalogue, then," said Shyamala coolly, looking him straight in the face, trembling slightly with what appeared to be barely restrained fury.

"Shyamala...," Nada began hesitantly, in a voice touched with concern.

In an instant, Shyamala raised the flashlight and struck Nada on the head, its beam swinging crazily from ceiling to floor. Then Shyamala dropped the flashlight and savagely hurled herself on Nada. The two fell struggling, Nada shouting Shyamala's name, Saul jumping back in confusion. Shyamala was now sitting astride Nada, strangling her, her fingers pressing deep into the flesh of her neck.

And then, reaching them without visible movement, Amruteshvar was kneeling beside them, gently but firmly grasping Shyamala by the back of the neck, growling something in the strange archaic Kannada that Nada had heard him speak to the possessed rickshaw driver.

Shyamala writhed as if she had been struck a mortal blow, throwing her head back, letting go of Nada, who lay still, dazed, her hair wet with blood.

The pale glow of the tube lights outside fell on Shyamala's face, which Nada saw dreadfully twisted with confusion and rage.

Amruteshvar continued to grasp her neck, and she

145

spasmed and grunted several times, her eyes turning up, then collapsed, vacated, on top of Nada, as Amruteshvar withdrew his hand.

Making no attempt to free herself, recovered from her brief swoon, Nada lay caressing Shyamala's shoulders and head, and before long Shyamala began to weep softly. For Nada, there was nothing to forgive: from the moment that Shyamala had struck her, Nada had known.

"He could take any one of us, any time," whispered Saul, still standing by the manuscript open on the desk, his eyes darting about.

"He won't attempt it again," replied Amruteshvar, not whispering. "Shyamala was the most vulnerable. She knew the least and had never been entered before. If he comes again, he must come as himself. Saul, you can easily find the manuscript."

Picking up the flashlight, Saul walked over to the cabinet with the C manuscripts, and Amruteshvar rose to follow him. Saul opened the door and slowly moved the beam over the paper labels one by one, got down on his haunches to reach the lowest shelf, then stopped.

"Here," he said, gently working a bundle out from under two others.

Amruteshvar was right next to him, a look of barely controlled impatience and eagerness on his usually impassive face, as Saul brought it to the table and untied it.

Nada had been sitting next to Shyamala on the floor with her arm around the younger woman's shoulder. She now stood, came over to the table, opened the pile of palm leaves to the final chapter, slowly added page after unbound page to the larger pile as she sought the critical verse.

na śastreṇa na śāstreṇa nihantuṃ śakyate' mṛtaḥ

Not by weapon, not by lore can the undead be killed

Nada's face and Amruteshvar's registered the same shock and surprise.

The gap! The same gap! And then:

mumukṣuṃ śamayet tu tam

one can lay to rest him who longs for release.

"How...?" began Amruteshvar in a voice shaking with consternation and disbelief.

Nada had never seen him betray any emotion stronger than pity, amusement, or at the most a moderate anger, as on the day when he had encountered and battled his brother. Now his face was the image of outrage, with wide eyes and trembling mouth. "He... he got to this one too! *How did he get to this one?*"

Nada and Saul stood staring at him, as appalled as if Avinash himself had appeared before them soaked in blood and with body parts tumbling from his mouth.

Everything had depended on Amruteshvar, this

mysterious man—if he *was* a man—who had until this moment given every sign of knowing everything, past, present, and future, that they would need to know in order to defeat Avinash. Even if he was standing back to watch them discover the truth for themselves, Nada had never had any doubt that he himself knew it, and that he could always consent to waive this exasperating condition and simply tell them what they needed to know when it became obvious that it was beyond them.

Tonight, confronted with this unexpected deviation from some ancient narrative of which he had thought he was the master, he had revealed his own limited and fallible humanity. In an instant, they had become four mere humans awaiting the pleasure of the truly omniscient supernatural.

Hands slipped round Amruteshvar's throat from behind, and he disappeared into the darkness, from which sounds of voiceless, savage struggle now emerged.

Saul turned the flashlight in that direction. Its beam found Avinash and Amruteshvar on the stone floor between two rows of cabinets.

Avinash, clad like Amruteshvar in traditional attire, was astride him on his back with his hands around his neck, rhythmically pounding his brother's face against the floor.

Amruteshvar reached back with his left hand, caught Avinash by the throat, and swung him in an arc over his head, hurling him onto his back against the floor, then sprang to his feet and kicked him, sending him flying down the aisle and crashing into the desks and chairs against the opposite wall.

Saul turned to look for the women, who winced when the flashlight's beam fell upon them where they stood together, Nada with her arm around Shyamala's shoulders. He moved towards them, gesturing with his free hand that they should all stand near the desk with the manuscript, and wait there, within range of whatever protection its auspiciousness might afford. Because what would be the point of escaping, even if they could?

More sounds of violence and a thunderous crash arose from the darkness. In the dim light from outside, one cabinet was hurled against its neighbours, which in turn fell like dominoes.

Saul again shone the flashlight into the darkness. Half the room was strewn with fragmented wood and glass, manuscripts still bound and intact, others torn open and scattered. Scarcely visible, shadowy figures flashed in and out of sight like jets over a bombarded city. One of the windows instantaneously became a blasted confusion of glass and metal, the sound registering a moment later like a crash of thunder.

Then the air was filled with a leonine scream of indignation and surprise. A figure appeared out of nowhere amidst the chaos on the floor. It was Amruteshvar. Even in that pale light, even at a distance, even though he appeared identical to his brother in every other way, the humanness of his expression of defeat and despair distinguished him unmistakably from Avinash.

He lay on his back, blood gushing from huge wounds all over his body, oozing onto the shards of glass and soaking the red cloth and palm leaves around him in a widening circle. He stared straight upward with fully conscious eyes, breathing raggedly.

Saul and Nada approached slowly, stepping over wood, glass, palm-leaf pages, and cloth, leaving bloody footprints on the floor. Both were weeping by the time they had reached him. His chest had been shattered by a tremendous blow. Whatever else he had made of himself, whatever superhuman powers he might have acquired, Amruteshvar was also most certainly a man, and he was dying like one.

"Amruteshvar," whispered Nada, stooping and caressing his head.

The gaze he turned on her was filled with a love and concern she had never perceived in him before. Her tears dripped onto his face, mingling with his blood.

He was trying to say something, phantoms of words flitted faintly under his rasping, bloody breaths. His eyes widened, then closed in resignation. Nada heard a faint sound behind her like the swishing of a garment, the clatter of something against the floor, then a dull thud of impact further away.

She turned and saw Saul lying slumped against the far wall in the lunar glow of the tube lights outside. The flashlight lay on the floor between them, shining into the empty darkness.

She cried out in alarm as hands emerged from

behind her, slipping under her arms, tightening under her breasts. Avinash's breath was on the back of her neck, she felt his lips and teeth laid against her skin, his smile as he inhaled at last the fragrance of her unbound hair, dropped his hands to caress her thighs, pressed himself fully against her from behind.

The nausea of utter terror flooded her. She flew into a fury of self-preservation, striking back with her elbows, reaching with both hands and grasping for his head. He growled, pressed his hands against her shoulders and thrust her forward. She staggered a few steps and collapsed face-down, and he hurled himself on her again. Astraddle on her buttocks, he seized her by the hair and nape, yanking back her head as she resisted him with every muscle, oblivious to any pain.

Again she felt the heat of his mouth on her cheek, heard a confusion of emotions in his snarling breath. He wrestled her onto her back and slammed her to the floor, and now she could see his face. He was weeping, his tears mingling with the network of blood that trickled from his clumped and glistening hair. His fanged mouth was twisted into a ghastly amalgam of triumph, mockery, fury, and anguish. He sat high astride her, looking down on her, paused as if hesitating, as if contemplating her.

Blood dripped copiously onto her from deep wounds to his head and body, bloody tears dripped into her eyes and mouth and mingled with her own. Because she was weeping too, weeping with pity and rage for the cyclic tragedy in which they were imprisoned together, in which the only act of love now left to her was self-surrender to her beloved's corrupted passion.

And in an almost visible flash of insight, they came to her, the missing words:

tasyā'rthāya hutātmai'va

only one who has sacrificed himself for his sake

hutātmā! "One who has sacrificed himself"! So this was the missing verse:

na śastreṇa na śāstreṇa nihantuṃ śakyate' mṛtaḥ
tasyā'rthāya hutātmai'va mumukṣuṃ śamayet tu tam

Not by weapon, not by lore can the undead be killed; *only one who has sacrificed himself for his sake* can lay to rest him who longs for release.

She realized that this was right, and that this was what she wanted. She had had enough of being harassed and thwarted by the motiveless malice of this stranger who had invaded her lover and warped his love only because he had cherished her too passionately, this intruder who in lifetime after lifetime, for the better part of a millennium, had destroyed their destined happiness by keeping them from knowing each other. She wanted her suffering to end, even if it meant her death. She wanted his suffering to end, even if it meant life without her. And she wanted their tormentor to be destroyed.

She arched her back and raised her throat to him, her eyes serenely closed.

There was a profound silence and stillness. She opened her eyes, and saw Avinash still staring down at her. An expression of astonishment had flooded his face, driving all malevolence from it, rendering it more human than ever before, despite the red eyes and bladelike fangs. They paused motionless in their joined position. He shuddered and jerked backwards as if the very sight of her lying self-surrendered beneath him were an overwhelming blast of wind or a flash of invisible light. His eyes closed in rapture or agony. He was trembling, suspended, unbreathing. Invisible hands seemed to shake him by the shoulders as he slipped from their grasp. The air was filled with a searing, inhuman scream that seemed to originate not from him but from somewhere above him. And then he fell forward onto her, released.

Saul lay where he had been hurled against the wall. Shyamala was sitting on the floor with her arms round her legs, watching.

Avinash and Nada lay still, but breathing. Amruteshvar lay not far away, showing no sign of life except a trace of ebbing consciousness in his eyes. He was looking straight upwards, but the faint smile that flickered onto his lips showed that he had seen everything. He was *kṛtakārya*, one whose task is accomplished. He too had been released.

Saul and Shyamala rose unsteadily to their feet.

Avinash and Nada stirred. He raised his head and looked at her in wonder. She smiled in half-believing joy as she looked into his eyes, brown-irised, fully human. Blood and tears mingled on their faces.

They sat up slowly, still embracing, still staring into each other's faces, their understanding and memory flowing ever more fully. They turned to look at Amruteshvar, stood up, walked slowly towards him, hand in hand, as Saul and Shyamala likewise approached from where they had been standing.

Smiling serenely, moments from death, Amruteshvar looked up at them as they stood around him weeping. Tears were flowing from the corners of his eyes too, washing channels through thick blood.

He turned his gaze on Nada and Avinash.

"*Pāhi tām*," he said. *Take care of her.*

11

THE SHARED PATH

Nada looked up to face a terrifying, hopeless mess in the manuscriptorium. There was the chaos of destruction caused by the brothers' battle: the splintered cabinets and desks, scattered and blood-soaked manuscripts, broken windows. Worse, there was Amruteshvar's corpse: nothing could have manifested his humanity more clearly than the surprising fact that no final miracle caused his body to disappear into thin air at the moment of death, or undergo some other supernatural metamorphosis, as might have been expected.

Silently, as if by a wordless consensus, the four of them carried the body outside into the night and cremated it on a large pile of sticks that the groundskeepers had collected near the library's unused second entrance in recent days. Perhaps some fruit of Amruteshvar's *punya*, holy merit, was after all to be seen in the way the body was totally consumed without a trace by the flames, and maybe, too, in the fact that neither the noise of the battle nor the light of the blaze attracted any attention from the guard or the groundskeepers' colony—though this might well also have been because they thought the Institute was again under attack by some infuriated mob.

Nada and the others made no attempt to clean up the manuscript department, which would have been impossible anyway, but they did rewrap the *Amrutajijnasa*, leaving it on the table, since its shelf had been smashed in the battle. Then they locked the door of the south wing, locked Saul's room in the guest house (they found the door still open and the light still on), and walked back to *Yadnya*, where they all collapsed into sleep in the study, Nada and Avinash on the pallet, Saul and Shyamala on the floor.

In all this, Avinash was one of them. He worked wordlessly alongside them, stunned like them by the tragedy that had just occurred. He and Nada stayed close to each other, frequently sharing touches of tenderness and reassurance, acting as if they were resuming a whole lifetime that they had lived together before somehow being cruelly separated.

"Lata..." he said to her once, half-whispering, looking into her face with wonder, as if unbelieving, or afraid to believe. And she clasped his hand, and returned his gaze with the fearless assurance and love that she knew he needed to see.

"It's true," she said. "We're here."

The whole scene was so unreal that Saul and Shyamala didn't even seem to notice the bizarreness of Avinash's suddenly changed role. But in fact his presence among them now did not seem unnatural, since he was evidently an altogether different person from the monster who only minutes before had been intent on killing them all.

The most obvious mark of this change was his eyes, now brown, and fully human in the range of emotions they registered: wonder, fear, pity, remorse, love, tenderness, gratitude. His wounds were appalling, but apparently did not represent any serious permanent injuries, since other than a slight limp in his left leg, his movements were normal and unimpeded.

And the limp was emblematic of a more general change: he had lost the terrible magnitude, the aura of enormous superhuman strength and inhuman cruelty that he had had as a demon. Amruteshvar had died like a man. From now on, clearly, his brother would live and suffer as one. And one day he, too, would die.

After that night, Nada and Avinash began living together at *Yadnya,* lying low, and never leaving the house. Disoriented by the unreality of their bliss and the inconceivable events that had made it possible, they gave no thought to the future, immediate or distant, sinking into each other with the suicidal defiance of doomed fugitive lovers towards a hostile world that will soon come after them.

At first Kamala was horrified at the sight of Avinash, whose face had been seared into her memory on the night so many years before when he had broken into the house and cursed her husband with the disease that had ruined their lives and ultimately killed him.

Nada did not have to work too hard to persuade her: even though Kamala had never joined Nada and Dr. Kshirasagar in their translation of the *Amrutajijnasa,* they had never kept any secrets from her, and the three had always discussed the work as equals—and of course, on the night of the encounter in the manuscriptorium, Kamala had revealed that she had always known more than Nada realized, more even than Nada herself. So Kamala was easily able to understand what had happened in recent weeks, and that the Avinash with whom Nada was now so passionately in love was a fundamentally different being from the monster who had terrorized them all for so long—all, and no one more than Avinash the man.

"Of course you can be here," she said to him gently, on the first day, as he stood before her with Nada, his face suffused with an agony of inexpressible guilt. "Anyone who loves Nada is forever welcome in our house." And Nada had laid her hand comfortingly on his shoulder, and looked at Kamala with silent gratitude.

Although Avinash's humanity was now obvious in every way, the nature of his particular human character remained, as yet, unknown.

Except to Nada. Nada knew him, and had known him, really, for twenty-five years in this lifetime alone, since Dr. Avinash Chandrashekhar had not been merely the puppet of Manyu the possessing spirit. This was the mystery of the thing: that Manyu, Rage (like King Nala's

Kali, Confusion), had been both self and other, both own and alien—just like any human passion, but more so.

When King Nala wavered again and again between abandoning and staying with Damayanti, the wife whom he loved and whose life he had destroyed along with his own, he was struggling with the Confusion that had possessed him. But his confusion was real, and it was his. Likewise, Avinash's cruel infatuation with Nada and murderous jealousy of Zoran were not so much false impositions on a helpless human host as demonically distorted and exaggerated forms of true love.

In the weeks when Nada was working with Amruteshvar and Shyamala on the translation of the *Amrutajijnasa*, her increasingly vivid dreams began to humanize Avinash and illuminate the tragic paradox of the *vetala* that the text described. During the long gap between Avinash's hijacking of the bus and his reappearance in the manuscript department, he became real enough for Nada to fall in love with him. She realized that this love was the re-awakening to consciousness of a passion that she had first felt when she was Lata, but her subjective identification with her ancient original took more time, deepening over the weeks as her story appeared to her again and again in a more and more integrated and literal form.

And other tragic love stories began to break through in flashes, which she knew must also be hers and Avinash's, in other incarnations over the centuries. Though her identification with these was even murkier, they overwhelmed her with a vertiginous sense of the depth of time and fate behind their love, and of the inexorability of the evil that had seized Avinash.

Since the moment of that evil's expulsion, the flow of memory had been increasing hour by hour. By now, she simply was Lata, fully and consciously, and was rapidly recovering countless other persons she had been over the centuries, and other Avinashes she had hopelessly loved.

For him, she knew, the recovery was different, a re-claiming rather than a recollection: he had been fully conscious of the whole centuries-long history since his adolescence, but that memory, like his whole person-hood, was experienced as something not quite his own, obscurely withheld from him by some alien occupier whose face he had never seen but whose silently threat-ening authority he had always felt. With the evaporation of that authority, he had, with violent immediacy, come into sole ownership of a self which spanned the better part of a millennium.

The change of perspective was terrifyingly disorient-ing, and he seemed to cling all the more to their love as the one great sure fact in his life. They hung on to each other, as he struggled to accept responsibility for an of-ten terrible legacy of actions for which he had not been fully responsible at the time, and she was buffeted by wave upon wave of returning lifetimes which threatened to sweep her into madness.

"Lata... *Nada*," he would say to her, anguished, "tell me again... that it's over, that we're together again, for-ever. And tell me... that it wasn't me... that it wasn't really me, alone, who did those terrible things, to you, to everyone."

And she would reply, kissing his cheek, "Avinasha... *Avinash...* We haven't been ourselves for so long. It wasn't your fault. It wasn't our fault, or if it was, it was so long ago, so many lifetimes ago, that no one could blame us for it. We've suffered enough. We are who we are."

The easy part was explaining their new relationship to others: they were simply a couple of indologists who had known each other professionally for many years and had in the natural course of events fallen in love. Nada's parents, who were only vaguely familiar with her professional life and had heard nothing specific about a Dr. Avinash Chandrashekhar, were very happy to hear that she had finally reached the far shore of her long mourning for Zoran and allowed herself to love again.

Indological friends who had seen something of her nasty relations with Avinash over the years were merely amused by the news of their liaison and engagement, since the development of a professional rivalry into a passionate affair was hardly unknown or psychologically inexplicable.

Saul and Shyamala, of course, were different: they had in effect been the witnesses at Nada's incredible marriage, and had thereby become her deepest intimates, a natural culmination of her lifelong friendship with Saul and her new one with Shyamala.

As for Avinash's relatives, they seemed to wonder what

Nada had done to him: he had always been such an asshole before, and now, overnight, he wasn't. But his dramatic transformation was easily understood as the natural effect of a great love, and Nada was accordingly welcomed with a warmth that a conservative Karnataka Brahmin family would not otherwise have granted to such an appallingly unconventional choice of bride on the part of their difficult son—even if she was a self-described "intellectual Hindu convert" and could easily "pass" in a sari and more than hold her own in Sanskrit conversation with the most learned of them.

There was also the supernatural rapidity with which she attained native fluency in Kannada, which could not really be fully explained by the fact that she was now using it more than she had ever had the opportunity to do before.

"It's kind of like I'm remembering it from a past life," she would say, laughing, when they expressed their astonishment and admiration. And Avinash would smile and look down.

Avinash's announcement that he would finally seek a permanent position as a Sanskrit professor—which he was certain to win easily either in India or the West—consoled his parents for years of professional waywardness in which he had squandered his dazzling gifts and achievements on aimless postdocs and promising assistant professorships that he had abandoned before allowing himself to take root.

Despite the unexpectedness and lateness of her

request, the University of Zagreb was more than happy to grant Nada a sabbatical year, given that she had never requested one before, being a notorious workaholic with no apparent personal life.

By the standards of academia, Avinash and Nada were still young and beautiful enough to be the superstar couple of their field. Yet their plan was to combine their resources so that they could wind down their careers to the minimum and spend as much time as possible together. Because already, though only in their forties, they were worn out with their indescribable secret tragedies and sufferings, and ready to make an early retirement to the nearest viable equivalent of life's final restful *ashrama*—a word that means both a hermitage and a stage of life.

If Avinash were to get a professorship somewhere in Europe, Nada could continue to work at the University of Zagreb in the downgraded role of assistant professor, which would allow her to stay with him most of the time, travelling to Zagreb perhaps once a week. She had a modest house in the Croatian countryside that she had inherited from her grandmother, and they would find another near his native Bengaluru. And Nada knew they would always be welcome at *Yadnya* in Pune. Kamala would always be family: indeed, Avinash and Nada were almost the only family she had.

Thus, they could keep one foot in each of their homelands, dividing the year between Europe and India, as Nada had done throughout her professional life. And they were both ready for such a division of labour:

unlike Avinash, Nada had had a steady academic career throughout her adult life, and being single and parsimonious, had already saved almost enough to retire, while Avinash's career, and even his life, were in a sense just beginning. Yet even he saw academic work as more of a necessity than a vocation, and Nada knew that he looked forward, like her, to shifting his professional focus from research to the less intellectually engaging duty of teaching.

"Yeah, I somehow feel that we've both perhaps had enough of research on obscure ancient texts and forgotten histories," she said once, explaining their plans to his family, and she and Avinash laughed, while their listeners smiled uncertainly, puzzled by their secret humour. At this point, their real heart's desire was to share what they knew and loved, reading beloved books like the *Mahabharata* and *Ramayana* together. And maybe, too, there were even books for them to write together. They both felt within themselves a vague stirring of something that they would eventually need to say, and not in the international English of the academy. Something inspired by their own *itihasa*, their own history, perhaps. Something, perhaps, like their own tale of King Nala and Damayanti.

As Nada eventually came to understand, Avinash's relatives were all the more inclined to rejoice in the salvation of their lost son because they were at the same time dealing with a harrowing tragedy that perfectly counterbalanced it: the disappearance without a trace of his brother Amruteshvar.

Through various embarrassed allusions and accidental references on the part of family members, Nada and Avinash eventually figured out that on the day before the showdown in the manuscriptorium, Amruteshvar had sent a devastating email, in Kannada, to his parents. Nada and Avinash insisted that they be allowed to read it, and this was reluctantly granted to them.

> *I have heard of my brother's outrageous decision to marry a foreign woman. This, for me, is the limit.*
>
> *I do not understand why my consistent lifelong devotion to my family and my duty has never won me the concern that you have always shown for my irresponsible—and, frankly, demonic—brother. I admit that he has always been more dynamic and charismatic than me, but this dynamism is superficial, and smells of evil, and the superior giftedness it seems to reflect is illusory.*
>
> *Why has my extraordinary career as a traditional scholar and an academic always been implicitly compared to his fragmentary achievements, and found wanting? I have sacrificed to my work even the legitimate possibility of marriage, while he has notoriously corrupted himself with unacceptable women both Indian and foreign. And now this.*
>
> *I know only too well how this announcement of his marriage will be greeted: with relief and celebration. But I will not be joining in the celebration this time, as in the past when everyone has rejoiced at each of his*

new undertakings as a hopeful first step towards self-rehabilitation. This is the end of my self-abnegation on behalf of my unworthy twin, who has always capitulated to a dark side that I have turned away from with natural ease.

I have never lacked for professional opportunities, and have repeatedly turned down lucrative offers to perform rituals for rich diasporic Hindus in America because of the contaminating effect that travel outside of the country would have on me in the eyes of our family's large conservative element—an effect that, again, my brother has largely escaped. Now, I will not hold myself back any longer. I will go to America, perhaps even marry.

In any case, it is no longer any of your business. You will never hear from me again.

Reading this, Nada felt a searing pity for the Chandrashekhars, who were clearly still as traumatized by this brutal loss of one son as they were overjoyed at the unbelievable recovery of the other which followed immediately after. Amruteshvar's farewell had taken them completely at unawares, but in retrospect, Avinash and Nada could see that he had been preparing the groundwork for this disappearance for years—and perhaps it had also been simply the inexorable working-out of his nature and destiny, as with Avinash. Nada's new family told her that they now remembered how Amruteshvar had again and again complained bitterly of the unfairness of the double standard by which he and his brother were so unequally judged. In recent years he had also often mentioned his research into the possibility of living as a performer of rituals in America, and issued veiled threats to make the move that he must now have actually made.

In a sense, Amruteshvar had not died, either literally or through self-exile. In this birth, as in all their previous ones going back to the beginning, everyone had seen the brothers as two facets of the same man, gifted in the same ways and to the same degree, the difference being that Avinash's nature was touched with fire, with an edge of intensity that constantly threatened to destabilize him, but which also carried the possibility of a nobility which Amruteshvar had always resentfully felt to be just beyond his grasp. But in death he had attained it, ennobling not only himself, but both of them. In the reborn Avinash, both Amruteshvar's steadfast goodness and Avinash's fierce brilliance realized and perfected each other at last.

And in fact, Nada and Avinash did not feel that Amruteshvar was gone. One day, as they sat together on plastic chairs in the small yard behind *Yadnya*, in the evening shade of the *ashoka* and mango trees, Nada said, stroking his hand, "You know, love, I sometimes wonder if, by sacrificing himself, he didn't just free the three of us from our tragedy. I wonder if he didn't free himself entirely— from the cycle of rebirth, the world of suffering and illusion. I wonder if it wasn't his *moksha*, his liberation. I mean, what he did... embodied and realized all his vast intelligence and insight..." (She felt her eyes shine with unshed tears.) "It wasn't just about the *vetala*. It was about life, about everything. It was the culmination of a great soul's struggle with existence."

And Avinash replied, "I... I think so too. But often... I also feel that somehow, at the same time, his individual consciousness has survived. I... I know you feel it too," he said, looking into her eyes, "I can feel that you feel it too—that he's somehow still here with us, around us, or... within me, that he's somehow merged with me, and that we've finally become the single person it always seemed that we ought to have been. That's how it feels to me. And such a thing is not unknown in the literature, the tradition. It's happened before."

"And anyway," she said, laughing, "nothing that has happened to us was possible. So anything is." She squeezed his hand, with a look of serious, deep feeling. "Yes. He's here."

Saul returned to his room the very next morning after the night in the scriptorium, and though he and Shayamala were able to report that the groundskeepers had cleaned up the mess, neither had heard anyone say a word about what was thought to have happened. Nor was anything reported in the newspapers.

A few days later, Nada emailed Vimala Bhave, ostensibly to tell her that the edition of the *Amrutajijnasa* was now complete, but really in the hope of learning something about the reaction to the scene of destruction they had left at the Institute. Vimala made no reference to it, beyond this possibly cryptic remark:

"This is happy news indeed, which marks the end of a long and difficult struggle for you and all those who have worked to solve the mystery of the *vetala*. May he rest in peace!"

Some days after they began to venture forth from *Yadnya*, Nada and Avinash went back to the Institute for the first time since that night. This was their furthest journey from the house thus far. At first they had not planned to end up there, but when they found that they had reached Tilak Institute Road, they realized that they were ready, and turned left towards the old hermitage.

When they got there, they sat on one of the benches in front of the library. It was a sunny, hot, beautiful post-monsoon day, but the rains had not yet stopped completely, and the grounds were still as luxuriantly green as they had been weeks before. Saul had long since vacated his room in the guest house and flown back to New York to prepare for the new academic year. Shyamala was now tutoring undergraduates at the university, and was not coming here as often. The few scholars and groundskeepers they saw from time to time came and went without noticing them.

After a time they got up and strolled arm-in-arm along the paved path. In front of the library's second, dis-used entrance, ash from Amruteshvar's funeral pyre was still visible on the pavement and ground. A gleam of light in the grass caught Nada's eye, and she stopped and bent to look.

It was Amruteshvar's ring. Jewelless and faded though it was, it was still a miracle that it had somehow not yet been found by someone else. Nada picked it up, and they wept together for the first time since that night. Deep and terrible as were the emotions that had buffeted them in the intervening weeks, it was not until now, in the vicarious presence of the tragic hero to whom they owed their love and freedom, that they had felt safe enough to let themselves go.

Avinash put the ring on, and they embraced. They knew that this had been their last incarnation apart, and that nothing would ever separate them again. At some time in the inconceivable future, events in a shared life they could not now imagine would bring them hand-in-hand to the final liberation that awaits all souls. But for now, the one they were living at this moment was as good as forever.

GLOSSARY

Words are Sanskrit unless otherwise stated. The common romanized form of most words is followed by a more precise transliteration with diacritical marks, which are only occasionally used within the novel's text.

akshamala (akṣamālā): "necklace of eleocarpus seeds", a sacred, auspicious object

amṛta (pronounced *amrut* or *amruta* in Marathi): "immortal, not dead"; also the name of the divine nectar of ancient story

Amrutajanmakatha (Amṛtajanmakathā): "Story of the Birth of the Nectar", a fictitious Sanskrit text

Amrutajijnasa (Amṛtajijñāsā): "Inquiry into the Undead", a fictitious Sanskrit text

ashoka (aśoka): a tree common in Maharashtra

ashrama (āśrama): "hermitage"; also one of the four stages of life of traditional Hindu thought (of which the third is retirement to a hermitage)

Avinashalatacharita (Avināśalatācarita): "The Story of Avinasha and Lata", a fictitious Sanskrit text

171

bhel (bheḷ) (Marathi): a popular snack food

bhut (bhūt) (Marathi): "ghoul, ghost"

brahmamuhurta (brahmamuhūrta): "the holy hour", the last period of night before dawn

desh (deś) (Marathi): "country, nation"

dosha (doṣa): "fault, sin"

Ganapati (Gaṇapati; Gaṇpati in Marathi): an elephant-headed god, also known as Ganesha *(Gaṇeśa)*

gav (gāv) (Marathi): "village"

gore (Marathi): "white person" (in the insulting neuter form, so "whitey")

gori (gorī) (Marathi): "white woman"

hutatma (hutātmā): "self-sacrificing", a martyr

idli sambar (idlī sāmbar) (Marathi): a popular snack food

Kadambari (Kādambarī): a Sanskrit novel by Bāṇa, renowned for the difficulty of its style

Kali: "Confusion" or "Destruction", a divinity

Kaliyuga: "Age of Confusion or Decline", the last and worst of the four ages of Hindu cosmology

kamarupi (kāmarūpī): "changing form at will"

kokil (kokiḷ) (Marathi): the "Indian cuckoo", a bird with an exuberant, laughing cry

lingam (liṅgam): a phallic idol

Mahabharata (Mahābhārata): a Sanskrit epic

makad (mākaḍ) (Marathi): "monkey"

Manyu: "Rage", a fictitious divinity

maushi (mausī) (Marathi): "maternal aunt, auntie", a common term of respectful address to an older woman *moksha (mokṣa):* "release, liberation"

Nala and Damayanti (Damayantī): a king and queen who are the subject of a famous story in the *Mahabharata*

namaskar (namaskār) (Marathi and Hindi, from Sanskrit *namaskāra):* a common greeting, "hello"

nishachari (niśācārī): "night-walker", a demon

Pandavas and Draupadi (Pāṇḍava, Draupadī): the five princes and their common wife who are the protagonists of the epic *Mahabharata*

pandita (paṇḍita): "learned man, scholar", an expert in traditional Sanskrit learning

panditya (pāṇḍitya): "scholarship, learning"

pret (Marathi): a reanimated corpse

punya (puṇya): "religious merit"

rakshasa (rākṣasa): "demon"

Ramayana (Rāmāyaṇa): a Sanskrit epic

shloka (śloka): "verse, couplet"

vatavaghul (vaṭavāghūḷ) (Marathi): a fruit bat

Veda: the fundamental sacred writings of Hinduism, constituting a large and various body of texts

vetala (vetāla): a vampire- or zombie-like supernatural being, variously described in various Sanskrit texts, but generally considered to be neither properly living nor dead

Vetalajyotsna (Vetālajyotsnā): "Moonlight of the Vampire", a fictitious Sanskrit text

vetalaraja (vetālarāja): "king of vampires"

vetalashastra (vetālaśāstra): "the lore, science, or study of vampires"

Vetalaviveka (Vetālaviveka): "Definition of the Vampire",
a fictitious Sanskrit text

Yadnya (Marathi form of Sanskrit *yajña*): "sacrifice,
act of worship or sacrifice", name of the house of
Professor Suresh Kshirasagar

ACKNOWLEDGEMENTS

I want to thank my friend Darryl Sterk for buying me this laptop at Vijay Sales in Pune with the express purpose of enabling me to write this novel, and for then passing on the manuscript, on his own initiative, to Linda Leith. I thank Linda for giving the novel a chance. And I thank her and Kodi Scheer for guiding me in putting it into a publishable form.